This special signed edition of
TORN
is limited to 750 numbered copies.

This is number ___494___.

TORN

TORN

LEE THOMAS

CEMETERY DANCE PUBLICATIONS

Baltimore
❖ **2012** ❖

Novella Series
Book 23

Cemetery Dance Publications
132-B Industry Lane, Unit #7
Forest Hill, MD 21050
http://www.cemeterydance.com

First Limited Edition Printing

ISBN-10:   1-58767-265-0
ISBN-13: 978-1-58767-265-1

Cover and Interior Artwork © 2012 by Vincent Chong
Interior Design by Kate Freeman Design
Dust Jacket Design by Desert Isle Design

Dedicated to Mike Hall and Jack Landers,
two guys who aren't torn at all.
And to JCP.

1

*How do you go on when something like that
happens to your child?*

Maggie Louise Mayflower, eleven years old and just as sweet as Christmas candy, left her house on a cool cloudy afternoon. She was going to the park with her best friend Emily from across the street. As always, Maggie promised her mother that she would stay away from the woods, promised to check both ways before crossing the intersection at Whitehall Street, promised she would be home in time to wash her hands for supper.

She didn't come home.

Not at six when the noodle casserole was done to a bubbly brown. Not when the sky turned dark thirty minutes later. Though more curious than concerned, Maggie's mother called Emily's house to see if her daughter was there, perhaps still playing and too distracted to remember her supper. Emily's mother felt certain that her own daughter was home, had heard the door to her bedroom close nearly an hour before. But when she went to see if Maggie was there, Emily broke into tears. She cried and whimpered, "I can't tell."

That's when Les Mayflower, Maggie's father, called me.

His call came while I was sitting with my own daughters. Gwen and Dru were doing their homework at the dining room table, as they always did. If I was home from the station, I sat with them and helped them a bit. Gwen was ten years old and Dru just eight, and like most parents, I saw miracles in their every accomplishment.

They did well in school, were behaved in public. Gwen liked to read and Dru liked to draw pictures, horses mostly. (If I had a nickel for every time she swore she'd "die if I don't get a pony," I might just have had enough money to buy her one). Gwen was happy with her *Harry Potter* books and the *Chronicles of Narnia* and liked to tell her sister that only "babies want ponies."

I imagine they got their artistic interests from their mother. Lisa used to sing and play guitar with her friend, Molly, at a bar up in Marrenville. That's where I saw my wife for the first time; that's where I fell in love with her. Both women were talented, but everyone recognized Lisa as the star of the act. You couldn't help but see it. Molly shared the stage but all but disappeared in the spotlight, whereas Lisa shined, drank in the attention and the accolades and then projected them back on the entranced audience.

While I guided the girls through math problems, their mother was upstairs, in bed, sleeping through one of her "migraines." My wife had a way with euphemisms.

TORN

My girls were arguing over the proper color pen to use to write down their homework answers when the phone rang. I answered quickly so the ringing didn't wake up Lisa—though little could wake her once she'd settled into her ministrations—and carried the phone with me into the kitchen.

"Bill," Les Mayflower said with a clipped bark. "Maggie's gone missing."

Well, you hate hearing something like that. My stomach dropped straight down to my shoes when I heard the news. Certainly what I felt was only a fraction of what Les was going through.

He was a fireplug of a man with a thick wave of salt and pepper hair and forearms as big as Popeye's. I pictured him pacing in tight laps, phone clamped to his head, the other hand worrying its way through his hair. I also imagined that his wife, Viv, stood next to him, maybe clutching one of his burly arms, her eyes already veined and wet from crying.

"Now, hold on," I said. "When was she last seen?"

"Viv said she went out a couple of hours ago, said she was going to meet Emily Salem from across the street. They were going to the park. But Emily's been home for a while now, and Maggie's still not here."

"What does Emily say?"

"Her mother couldn't get a word out of her. She just broke down crying and screaming, and that don't strike me as normal, Bill. Now, you know I wouldn't bother you if I wasn't certain we had trouble."

"I know, Les. Did you go over to the park?"

"Not yet. I'm heading there the second I hang up this phone. I didn't want to waste any time getting word to you,

9

especially after the way little Emily carried on. Sounds like she's scared to death if you ask me."

"Sounds that way. Did you call the station?"

"No. I called you first, figured it would cut out the middleman."

The middleman to whom Les referred was one of my deputies, Duke. He was a thirty-four year old country boy who was as cultured as a chicken coop, with a temper that went from fine-by-me to say-your-prayers in about one second flat.

"Good thinking, Les," I said. One of my daughters shrieked from the next room, and my stomach did another plunge. The round of trilling giggles that followed eased my nerves only slightly. "I want you to go on over to the park and see if you can't find Maggie. I'll have my phone with me. In the meantime, I'm going to have Duke make some calls, see if we can't get a few of the boys out looking. I'm going to stop on by the Salem place, try and get some sense out of Emily. Then, I'll go have a chat with Viv."

"Thanks, Bill," he said. "I hope I'm just overreacting."

I wish he had been.

These are cruel times, I'll admit. But all times are cruel; most just don't get so much press. We have the nightly news, using everything from terrorists to carbohydrates to scare the shit out of us, and they love to draw X-es over the eyes of innocent faces. A child's terror, a parent's misery, are good for the ratings. So every time we hear about a kid that doesn't come home for dinner we remember the others: the girl snatched from her driveway by a handyman; the girl taken from her bed by the "quiet" old man down the street; the pretty child dragged into the brush by a stranger. We can't help but remember them.

As a father, those kinds of stories were carved into me, but I never expected to be facing one in my own backyard.

It took me a few minutes to wake Lisa. She mumbled and rolled away from my touch. Her "migraines" were becoming more frequent. I tried to be patient, but the scratch of frustration at seeing her this way was with me a lot. Every time one of the girls asked, "Is mommy sick?" it felt like a punch in my gut. I grasped Lisa's shoulder real tight and gave it a good shake. When her eyes opened and seemed like they might stay that way for more than a second, I told her to throw on some clothes and get downstairs.

"You need to watch the girls. I have to go out."

"I'll bet," Lisa muttered, wiping at her mouth with the back of her hand. She shot me a cutting glare and blinked. My wife looked around the room, dazed, then back at me. "What are you doing home so early?" she asked, as if I'd just walked into the room.

"Get dressed," I said, no longer worried about upsetting her. "Put on your clothes and get downstairs. I don't have time to argue with you. Maggie Mayflower is missing, and I don't want Dru and Gwen going out until we know what happened. They'll need some supper. I'll leave money for a pizza. Now, hurry up. I have to leave."

"Don't want to keep *her* waiting," she said with a voice as bitter as it was garbled.

I shook my head and left the room. For the last year or so, Lisa's accusations had gone from casual, nearly joking, to outright hostile. They were ridiculous, and I wasn't going to stand around trying to defend myself against a pill-fueled delusion. I had more important things to worry about.

I pulled into the Salems' driveway, still fuming over Lisa's behavior. After parking, I just sat behind the wheel for a minute, letting the steam in my head dissipate a bit. I didn't want to carry too much frustration in with me when I questioned little Emily. The last thing either of us needed was for me to lose my temper.

Dick Salem greeted me at the door with a strong handshake and a serious expression. He had the narrow face and flat chin of a Saxon, with a sweep of auburn bangs like the wing of a robin draped across his brow.

"Has she said anything?" I asked, letting go of Dick's hand.

"No, Sir," he said, as if he was a subordinate officer. "She's in a state, and I didn't have a bit of luck."

He invited me in and led me across the living room. The impeccably clean house, the new furniture, the attention to warmth and hominess, reminded me of what my own home was missing, and my thoughts drifted back to Lisa's doped stare. She'd been beautiful once, intelligent and talented. Those days were gone. That woman was gone, replaced by a suspicious wife and a failing mother, who insulated herself with pills.

I followed Dick down a brightly lit hallway, decorated with two dozen family photographs in neat, wooden frames.

"She saw something," Dick said of his daughter. "We know that. She said she promised not to tell, said she was scared. So, we know she saw something. Talked to somebody. Duke called about five minutes ago, so I'm on my way out to help with the search, but Olivia will be here. You just let us know what needs to be done."

"You go on ahead. See if you can't catch up to Les at the park. If he's not there, just drive up and down Whitehall."

Dick stopped in the hall and turned on me. "You think it's one of those molesters?" he whispered. "You think we got one of those bastards in town?"

"I don't know what to think yet, Dick. Let me see what Emily has to say."

"Yes, Sir."

He pushed open the door, and Emily flinched. She lay on the bed, curled up knees to chest. Her large blue eyes erupted with fear and then calmed upon recognizing her father.

"Emily," Dick whispered, "this here is Sheriff Cranston. You remember him from the church picnic at Labor Day?" Emily didn't respond. She just stared at us both, trembled. "Well, he's going to ask you some questions, sweetheart. I want you to try and answer him, okay?"

No response.

What I had in my head was that someone had approached both Emily and Maggie. He decided he was going to snatch Maggie, and, to buy himself time, he put some deep dark fear into Emily. Any adult would ignore such a threat, but Emily was a little girl who'd just had her first encounter with a real life monster. It was no wonder she doubted her safety.

I approached the bed slowly, crouched down, smiled as pleasantly as I could.

"You know you're not in any trouble, don't you?"

I detected a slight movement of her head. Yes, she understood.

"And you know that nobody is going to hurt you. You know that you're safe, don't you?"

13

No response.

"You met someone kind of mean today, didn't you? I'll bet he said that if you told your parents what you saw something bad was going to happen. Maybe to you. Maybe to your parents. Maybe to Maggie. But he wasn't telling the truth, Emily. He was a liar. The only way he can do something bad is if you don't tell us what happened. You know that don't you?"

No response.

"Okay," I said. "I'll bet he didn't say anything about me guessing what happened, did he?"

Emily shook her head rapidly. When she realized what she had done, the sparkle of fear returned to her eyes.

"That's okay. If I guess what happened, it's not your fault. So, I'm going to guess that it was a man who said those bad things to you." Her chin dipped slightly toward her chest. "And he took Maggie away in his car."

No response.

"He didn't drive? He walked away?"

Her chin dipped again.

"Did he take her down Whitehall? Up Whitehall? No. Did he take her toward the woods on the far end of the park? I'll bet he did, didn't he?"

Her chin dipped.

From above, the city of Luther's Bend looks like an eye, due in part to the city circle in the middle of town and the wetlands to the west where the river cuts a sharp angle across one marshy edge and a stand of conifers angle in from the south. To the east, Wilhelm Mathers Park fans out from a thick forest of pine and spruce, looking like a teardrop floating sideways. At the point of that teardrop is what's called The Den. Late at night, rebellious kids from unfortunate homes meet under the jutting forest cover to smoke dope, snort meth, drop acid and drink whatever spirits they'd managed to steal. The broad end of the park, the one running along Whitehall Road, is neat and well kept, suffering none of the litter or abuse inflicted on The Den. A new playground was erected a few years back, far enough from the street to keep curious toddlers from having easy access to passing car bumpers. Like most playgrounds, it has a set of swings, a jungle gym with a deep pad of sand below, a teeter-totter, a merry-go-round and a kind of treehouse that only stands five feet off the ground. Thick plastic tubes run from the main structure of the fort, curling and arcing like intravenous tubes.

This was where Emily Salem and Maggie Mayflower would play together for the last time.

After getting what information I could from Emily, I instructed Olivia Salem to take her daughter to the emergency clinic on the north end of town. Emily was suffering from shock and should be checked over by Dr. Laughlin. Then I called Duke and told him to round up whomever he could and meet me at the east end of the park.

"Ed can watch the station. I'm going over to the Mayflower place to get a picture of Maggie from Viv. Bring flashlights and the talkies. Get on the horn to the state police and let them know we have a kidnapping, probably a youth sex offender. Caucasian. Approximately six feet. The guy is probably in his fifties, could be older. Slender build. Brown eyes."

That was the best description I could get from Emily. After playing the guessing game for twenty minutes, feeling the distance spreading between Maggie Mayflower and me with every time-consuming question needling my chest, I took what I had and left. By the end of it, though I kept my voice steady and the smile plastered to my face, my frustration with Emily Salem was bordering on rage.

We'd lost too much time already.

I drove up Whitehall, my headlights cutting through the late evening gloom to fall across half a dozen cars parked at the curb. Another car pulled up behind me and Arthur Milton met me at the trunk of my car.

Arthur was a good enough guy, but he had a reputation in town that kept a lot of us folks at a distance. Arthur was a confirmed bachelor in a town that didn't quite understand the concept. Now, he wasn't queer or anything like that. No, he liked the women well enough, maybe too much, and he didn't let a little thing like wedding vows get in his way. Though mostly rumored, Arthur was said to have bedded a good number of married women and caused more than one divorce in his day.

"Arthur," I said. "Glad you could help out."

"It's not true, is it? I mean, it can't be true."

"We know that Maggie was led into the woods by a middle-aged man. That's about it right now."

"Dear Lord," he whispered, shaking his head.

I retrieved the halogen lantern from my trunk, tested it, cutting a thick white line through the night air. Satisfied, I closed the trunk and looked at Arthur, wondering as I always did in his company, how such an unremarkable looking fellow might have such luck with the ladies.

He was thickly built, though his gut wasn't spilling over his belt. Balding and blunt of feature, he wasn't an ugly man, but he wasn't likely to be mistaken for Casanova anytime soon either.

With Arthur on my heels, I set off toward The Den, where several flashlight beams were already sweeping the tree line.

"So, what's the plan?" Arthur asked.

"Well, I'll tell you, I don't know exactly. There's nothing but woods in those woods, and nothing for miles but more woods with nothing in them. We're just going to have to do a sweep, hope we can find a trail of some kind. No matter what happens, it's going to be a long night."

"Well, you got me for as long as you need me."

"Thank you, Arthur. We can use all the help we can get."

We padded over the soft grass until we met up with the men and women, ten in all, at the tree line. I knew them, of course. Duke's brother, Mel, was there, cradling a hunting rifle in his arm and looking every inch the persona of bad country heritage. His running buddy, Reed—also armed with a rifle, puffed on a cigarette and eyed me with suspicion as I approached. The one face I most expected to see, that of Les, Maggie's father, wasn't in the crowd.

"Where's Les?"

"He went on in the woods with Garrett Newman and his boys. Told us to tell you he was heading southeast."

Though I said, "good," I didn't mean it. The last thing I wanted was for Les to stumble across an ugly scene in which his daughter was involved. He shouldn't have to see something like that. No one should. Silently, I prayed that whatever was to be found in those woods, would be found by someone else.

"Okay, gather 'round," I said.

"We got a few other boys out there," Mel said, before spitting a foul dark wad of tobacco juice onto a discarded beer can. "Ha. Bullseye. But yeah, Ramsay and Baker went in about twenty minutes ago, too. Reed and I was just about to wade in, but Duke said we should wait on you."

"Good," I said. "First thing, no guns. You go into those woods, you leave the firearms behind. I don't want you boys shooting each other in the dark."

"What if the fucker's packing?"

"Then, you get out of there and call me up on your talkie."

"I ain't leaving my baby," Reed said, hefting his rifle.

"Then you can go on home. I appreciate the help, but we're playing by my rules. Understand?"

Reed scowled and let his baby droop at his side, its muzzle grazing over the lawn and clipping the beer can his buddy had spat on moments before.

"Okay," I said in as loud a voice as I could muster. "This is how it's going to work…"

"I'm glad you didn't let those boys bring rifles into these woods," Arthur said, trudging next to me. "They'd be shooting at every bug fart."

Arthur and I followed the path that I felt was the most likely. It cut straight back from The Den. Though narrow, the path was defined and easy to navigate, which I figured would make it attractive, at least initially, to a man I assumed wasn't familiar with the territory. Every twenty yards or so, we'd come across a broken branch or a displaced bed of needles that made me think we were on the right track. Despite this minor sense of accomplishment, nagging pessimism crawled on me like ants. Not only were the woods pitch black—the sliver of fingernail moon swaddled well behind thick clouds—but the forest went on for miles. Sure, the man might have dragged Maggie along this trail for a while to gain distance, but at any point he could have veered off, gone north or south, doubled back, and we wouldn't be any the wiser. And the noise Arthur pointed out added to the frustration. Branches snapped, logs settled, animals hunted and foraged. Insects buzzed and chirped. Add to that the tromping boots of a dozen concerned adults, bouncing off of tree trunks, echoing through the needles and brush, and I began to understand just how intimidating this particular haystack was.

"We don't want to make things worse," I said, responding to his comment about keeping the men unarmed. "If it were daylight, I might have a different feeling about it."

"Well, you did right."

I wondered if Arthur's worry went deeper. Who could tell which of the men in the party had a wife Arthur had known?

I cast a glance over Arthur's head, saw the distant sweep of a flashlight revealing thick tree trunks in silhouette on the rise. The beams looked tiny and insubstantial amid the vast, rolling darkness. My spirits withered and drooped.

We weren't going to find this guy unless he wanted to be found.

As it turned out, that's what he'd wanted all along.

We walked for over an hour before Arthur found the shred of cloth dangling from a nettles branch. The scrap was baby blue, the color of the cotton sweater Maggie was wearing when she disappeared.

"Okay, I'm going to get the boys over here," I said.

Arthur nodded, looking proud of himself and eager to continue the search. He did a quick turn, surveying the woods on all sides with a sweep of his shoulders and head.

I got on the talkie and told the search party to head toward my position. It didn't occur to me that few, if any, of the party knew where my position was. I hadn't thought in terms of coordinates or landmarks. I did the only thing I could think to do. I told everyone to look for my flashlight beam. I'd direct it up and get as many to me as possible.

"We'll wait for ten minutes and then move on," I said.

"We're just going to wait?" Arthur asked.

"For now."

"How about I go up a ways? I'll stay on the path. I won't go far. I just think we're getting close."

"That material could have been there for hours," I said, refusing to allow a break in my pessimistic hide. "It means they came through this way. That's all."

"I won't go but fifty yards," Arthur said.

"Okay," I told him. "But you stay on the path. If you get the slightest urge to go off of the path, you fight it, and you get your ass back here. The same goes for if you see or hear anything. We don't know if this man is armed."

"Good," Arthur said, so anxious to move on that he was dancing from foot to foot.

I imagined he was hoping to come out of this a hero with a story to tell his women. I didn't mean to be so uncharitable to Arthur, but the thought leapt into my head and decided to stay for a bit.

So, I stood there with my lantern aimed at the sky like a guy under a space ship's teleportation device, and Arthur took off down the path.

He wasn't gone a full minute before he started shouting.

TORN

◈

"She's here! Sheriff! Bill! She's over here."

I dropped my arm and was in a full sprint before the lantern's beam came horizontal. Branches scraped across my chest, tore at the sleeves of my jacket. The scene before me jerked and leaped as the light bounced from side to side. Ahead, I saw Arthur kneeling down by a pile of blue with what looked like two white sticks jutting from it. My heart beat too fast, my throat tensed, closed around a knot.

Maggie Mayflower was laid out on the path, her hands and feet bound together and secured to thick tent stakes, driven deep in the ground. I saw all of this long before I reached the little girl.

I never quite reached Arthur.

A flash of movement from the right startled me. I stumbled on the uneven trail and caught myself in time to see Arthur being carried away.

He screamed, his voice tearing through the forest, high and shrill. He sounded like a child himself. The peels of fear formed no words that I could understand, just one piercing cry after another. In the beam of my lantern, he seemed to be floating over the ground, his eyes and mouth wide while his arms and legs swatted and kicked. Of his attacker, I saw a muscled arm, wrapped around Arthur's midsection. Then a back and two powerful legs, pumping and stomping on the earth as he raced deeper into the woods, his struggling captive held with as little effort as a pillow or a doll. The man's size and strength exceeded the description little Emily Salem had given me, and I immediately considered the likelihood that the withered old man she'd described wasn't working alone.

In only a handful of seconds, Arthur was gone. Even the sound of his captor's trampling steps vanished.

Panicked, I raced forward and then remembered the child. I went back to Maggie Mayflower and nearly cried when I saw the recognition and life in her teary eyes. With my knife, I cut her free. Her mouth was gagged with a blue handkerchief. This I removed as gently as I could.

"Thank you," she whispered through a dry throat. Then, she lunged forward and wrapped her arms around my neck.

I held her, tried to soothe her. We stayed like that until the search party gathered on the path around us.

"Keep that blanket around her and get her to the clinic," I told Les. "Take Mel and Reed with you. Boys, once you see that Les and Maggie are safe in their car, I want you to grab your guns and haul ass back. Arthur is still out here."

"Did you see the guy that grabbed him?"

"Not well," I said. "He was big, though, and damned strong."

"I thought we were looking for a scrawny old guy," Reed said.

"That's what Emily Salem told me, but she may have had it wrong. That or we got two crazies out here. Either way, we're wasting time. Get moving. The rest of you come on ahead with me."

Flanked by Robert Dawson, a furniture builder; Harvey and Flo Becker, the owners of Luther's Bend's only hotel; Hank Allen, a mechanic; Dan Mott, a slender kid who just got out of the army; and Mark and Adrienne Golden, a couple of accountants who did just about everyone's taxes, including mine, I set off down the path.

As we walked between the dark tree trunks, I tried to form a clearer picture of the man that had dragged Arthur away. Quickly, I corrected myself. Arthur was not dragged away, he was carried. I remembered the arm, pictured the back, flexing with strain. Something about it was wrong, but the abduction had happened so quickly, it was hard to pinpoint the exact wrongness. Maybe it was the color of the skin, not quite Caucasian, certainly not African. I got to thinking about Latino and Asian, but the tone wasn't particular to those either. The skin was gray. I remembered the skin being the color of a rotten steak. More disturbing, I didn't see the man's head or face. They were far darker, perhaps hidden beneath a hood of some kind. Otherwise, the guy was naked. Bare assed naked.

A sick feeling gripped me as I led the group over the trail, my heart pulsing heavily every time my foot caused the pine needles to whisper. The feeling was fear, absolute terror. Arthur Milton was a big man, had a good amount of bulk on him. Anyone that could make such easy work of his weight was someone to worry about. It didn't help that we were surrounded by blankets of darkness, walls of undergrowth, the distracting sounds of a living forest.

A branch cracked ahead and to my left. I froze. Behind me, Flo Becker gasped. They shouldn't be here, I thought. Despite a profound hesitance to move forward with fewer people at my side, these folks were civilians. I shouldn't be putting them at any additional risk. Maybe I'm one of those chauvinists, probably so, but my greatest concern was for the women.

23

"Harvey. Mark. I want you to take Flo and Adrienne on back now. Thank you for your help, but this isn't a search anymore, it's a hunt."

All four of them looked relieved, and I didn't blame them for that one bit. Harvey opened his mouth to protest, but Flo was already grasping his arm, hauling him the other direction.

"You four stick together. Get on back to your homes as fast as you can and call Ed. Let him know how far in we are. Tell him I'll check in. If you see Duke or Mel and Reed, tell them to hurry it up."

Mark Golden nodded his head, grasped his wife's hand in his, and the four turned away, leaving me with Hank and Robert and Dan. The remaining men's faces were caught in the periphery of my lantern's beam, glowing like masks lit from behind.

"Your main concern is Arthur," I told them. "Capturing this asshole takes a distant second right now. None of you are trained, so I don't want you taking this guy on. You keep your thoughts on Arthur and let me worry about the perp. If he comes at you, get out of his way, defend yourself if you have to, but do not try and apprehend him. You got me?"

All three agreed, and I turned back to the path.

A thick scrub of nettle bushes and creeping vines blocked the trail. I played my light over the green barricade, looked for a break and realized we'd have to veer left or right. I checked the directions with the lantern's beam. Something shimmered against the trunk of a tree on my right, and I walked up to get a better look.

Amid the creases and dimples in the bark of a knotty pine, I found a series of glistening red smears. Blood. Though each was only the size of a nickel, hardly marks of a fatal wound, two of the stains were accompanied by ragged, cream colored shards. Arthur had clutched at this trunk, dug his fingers in. He left two fingernails behind, lodged in the rough bark.

My stomach flipped. I knew the direction we had to go; but God knows I didn't want to take it.

"Damn, Bill, are those…?" The question came from Dan Mott, the army kid.

"Yeah. Let's keep moving."

"Damn," Mott whispered.

The forest fell in tight around us. At our feet, roots rose, threatening to trip us or crack our ankles. The ground was pitted with divots, some nasty enough to cause a sprain if we didn't watch our step.

Goose pimples covered my skin. Actually, they'd been on me since setting off into the woods over an hour ago to find Maggie Mayflower. But they suddenly felt alive, like the nesting place for miniscule parasites, now awake and writhing.

I pushed a low hanging branch aside with my lantern, felt the sap on the back of my hand. I kept my service revolver pointed into the darkness ahead, holding it as steadily as I could manage. The branch snapped back, but Mott caught it. I directed my light ahead and froze.

I barely registered the naked man on the ground, my attention held by what knelt over him. This too might have been a man, but considering what I interrupted, I didn't want to believe it.

The beast had Arthur Milton's right pectoral clamped in its teeth. It shook and yanked at the skin and muscle, until the whole of it tore away with a wet snap, dappling the dead man's torso with freckles of blood.

It looked up at me then, a good portion of Arthur's chest hanging between sharp red-smeared teeth. Even then, I might have believed this thing to be a man. The body, incredibly built with bulges and knots of muscle was human enough, and the thick pelt of hair at its chest, trailing down its abdomen was common for men, but there was the issue of the skin's hue, gray like old meat.

And there was the face.

Pronounced ridges at the brow and along the cheekbones angled foreword, leading to a protrusion. A snout? A muzzle? Even as I looked upon the thing, I questioned its constitution. It was an impossible melding of species, part man and part…

Wolf? Dog?

I couldn't fit this creature into any of my mind's compartments; the only nooks available to it came from childhood spaces that had once accommodated fairy tales and monster movies, now old and filled with clots of dust.

My body was alight with energy as if connected to a low voltage wire. Behind me, Dan Mott screamed, and I began firing.

My first shot hit the thing's shoulder. The bullet passed through, spraying the woods with fluid and bits of skin. It sprang upward, dropping Arthur's chest meat onto the supine body it had been torn from. The second bullet went through its thigh. It roared, spun, disappeared into the forest. I kept shooting. Maybe I hit it again, maybe I didn't.

Hank and Robert and Dan were babbling like idiots, filling the wood with obscenities and prayers. They huddled around me. Hands clutched my shoulders, my arms.

"Knock it off," I said, shaking them off of me.

I stepped forward. Played my light over the forest to make sure the beast wasn't coming back for us. Then, I dropped the beam to Arthur Milton's naked and abused body.

All four of us took a couple of minutes to empty our stomachs in the bushes.

◇

"Werewolf."

Robert Dawson, the furniture maker, was the first one to say it. Maybe we were all thinking it, maybe it was just Bob and me, but as soon as I heard the word aloud, I realized how ridiculous it sounded, and I knew damned well I didn't want anybody saying it to the state boys when they arrived.

"Just a crazy in a mask," I said.

"You can't tear out hunks of a guy with rubber teeth," Hank said. "Hell, even I know that. Maybe we ought to give what Bob said some thought."

"Sweet Mary, mother of shit," Dan said, leaning back on the trunk of a tree. "A werewolf."

"Stop talking yourself into that crazy shit," I said.

"Into it?" Dan replied. "I'm trying to talk myself out of it, but what the hell else could it have been? Hank's right. Fake teeth can't do that to a man."

"You see a full moon?" I asked. "You see hair covering that guy? Below the neck he wasn't any different than a thousand other guys. And just so you know, my bullets don't have a scrap of silver in them."

"How many times did you shoot him?" Bob asked, thinking he had his trump card.

"I got him in the shoulder and the leg. Both flesh wounds."

"And it didn't slow him down a bit." This from Hank.

"Fine," I said. "If any one of you boys feels you need to tell the troopers about a wolf man, you go right ahead. I'll be sure to send flowers to your ward at the loony bin. My story is going to be a nut case in a mask."

This quieted them down, got them to thinking a little more rationally. It was one thing to throw that shit around among friends, but I don't think one of them was willing to risk their reputations to defend that particular fairy tale to state troopers or television reporters.

As for me, I started examining Arthur's remains, though I knew the state boys would be along shortly and could do a far more thorough and efficient job of it. I knelt down by his left shoulder, drew a line up his legs with my light. Both thighs were torn away, leaving broad ragged wounds. Blood pooled in these, so I suspected they occurred pre-mortem. The wound on the right leg was so deep, the femur was exposed, creating a ridge like a serpent surfacing in a red pond. I moved the light higher, leaving behind the grotesque wound and falling on his privates.

"I guess we know what made Arthur so popular with the ladies," Hank said.

"Damn," Dan Mott said. "I wonder if he had to burp that thing."

This got the three men laughing, but I wasn't having any of it. "Show a little respect for the guy."

They kept cackling like a bunch of hens. But they tried to keep it down.

I slid the light's beam over Arthur's belly, up to the wound on his chest. This was a drier wound with little pooling. The skin at its edges drooped like wet paper into the shredded striations of muscle. The wad of flesh that fell from the beast's mouth sat like a lump of clay on Arthur's sternum. Both of Arthur's biceps were similarly torn away.

Muscle meat, I thought. It went for the prime cuts.

Not *it*, I reminded. *He*. *He* went for the major muscle groups.

And he ate them. He'd chewed Arthur's quadriceps and his biceps and a pectoral and except for this last, which littered Arthur's chest, he'd swallowed them raw.

My stomach flipped again, and I stood up.

Behind me, the bushes erupted with sound. A wheezing pant joined the snapping of brush and I spun, my revolver already aimed at chest level. And I almost pulled that trigger, almost sent lead into the darkness, but something paralyzed my fingers.

Mel and Reed and my deputy, Duke, burst through the brush, all of them wild eyed, sighting down the barrels of their shotguns.

"We heard shots," Duke said. "You guys okay?"

2

I kept Mel and Hank with me, sent the others back to the trail to make sure the state boys found their way to us. Standing over Arthur's body, I felt like a frightened kid, my mind returning to the days when monsters were real and any dark place was likely to brim with them. Things moved in that darkness. Several times while waiting with the body both Mel and Hank spun toward a sound in the forest, only to whip back around because a new sound emerged on the other side of us. In those instances, you can't help but react. I too turned to the noises, gun raised, telling myself that Arthur's killer was coming back for seconds. When your nerves are that frayed, cruel imagination has the opportunity to peek through the holes, worry them and remove the threads so it can emerge to fill your head with any number of disturbing fantasies. At one point the subtle rustlings in the forest grew so frequent I thought we were being circled.

It was just the wind, I told myself. Foraging animals. Settling deadfall.

I spent a lot of time in these woods as a kid, playing games like tag and hide and go seek; building forts out of fallen branches and thick slabs of scabby bark; setting off in search of imaginary treasures. My best friends from those days, Timmy Feld and Nathan Holm and I hiked and hid and pretended battle beneath the pines. We found our own world there, a magical primeval world scented like a musky Christmas, a world for boys. I saw my first girlie magazine in those woods, took my first puff off of a cigarette and had my first sip of beer. But for all of the time spent and all of the adventures taken, the woods had never scared me before. As a boy, the woods seemed exactly the place I belonged.

Those joyful days were gone.

For all of my fond and familiar memories of this forest, I stood in it with Mel and Hank and the remains of Arthur Milton, feeling completely lost. The woods held no hidden treasures, no damsels to rescue; they were simply a dark and dangerous place, providing ample cover to at least one monster.

When the state boys showed up, they came stomping through the forest like a platoon, lights cutting the tree trunks and brush. I was relieved to see them. They walked onto the scene all good-natured authority and efficiency, gave Arthur a look, shook their heads. A couple of boys cursed, but none of them had the gut reaction we local folks had at seeing the gaps in Arthur's body. After all, the state boys spent their days scraping people out of ten car pile-ups, shoveling remains off the rocks at the base of Treetop Bluff (a popular place for suicides upstate). The destruction of the human body came in a number of fashions, and these boys had seen most of them.

They didn't have to say a word; the crime scene was theirs. When a big trooper with a close-shaved mustache asked me to stand back, I stood back. I didn't have an ounce of ego about it. Most of the dead bodies I'd seen were in training films and the occasional old folk whose hearts gave out in the middle of the night. The two murders that occurred in my town since I joined the police force were both gunshot victims. Neat. Clean. No mystery as to their killers. My life as Sheriff for Luther's Bend was an easy one, so I deferred to the state boys. They would do the job, and they'd do it right, at least, far better than I could.

I was taken aside by a young trooper named Burleson who wanted my version of the events, which I gave him, including the bit about a psycho in a mask. He looked skeptical, asked if it might have been an animal, and I assured him it was not.

"So we have the alleged child offender and this other guy," Burleson said.

"Yes. Unless that freak already made a snack of the offender."

"Is there any chance they are the same person?"

"Yes," I told him, explaining that my description could have been way off. After all, a very disturbed little girl had provided the only information I had. She might have remembered the incident wrong. "But if this is the same guy, why didn't he harm Maggie? He had her tied up for a good long time. A lot longer than he had Arthur, and he made quick enough work of him."

"Couldn't say," Porter replied. "Why don't you give me that description again?"

So, the night passed. The state boys set up lights and took pictures; they swept the area for evidence. Porter told me that they had an all points bulletin out with the description I gave him, but they wouldn't start searching the woods until morning when full light rose. Two hours before that dawn came the state boys zipped Arthur Milton into a black rubber bag.

I drove back to the station bone tired. Nothing was solved. No arrests made. At least one sick son of a bitch, maybe two, had come to town and for all I knew were still prowling the forest on its outskirts.

It was likely the sex offender had moved on (if he was a different guy than the one I saw taking apart Arthur). The killer might have spooked him after he finished tying Maggie Mayflower to the ground. If he was lucky, he fled a good long ways from my town. If fortune wasn't exactly pleased with his behavior, the state boys might just stumble over his butchered body once they began to sweep the forest. I didn't have a single bitch about that scenario.

But whether two monsters roamed our woods or just the one, the fact remained that Luther's Bend was going to be carrying fear for a good long time.

I entered the station and greeted the two deputies on duty. The station was small, with four desks behind a low wall that separated the reception area from my deputies' desks. The door to my office was on the right of the back wall, and the door to the holding cells was on the left. The corridor at the front of the building, which ran to the right, led to the restrooms, the locker rooms and shower, a storage closet for office supplies, another for weapons and a narrow shooting range at the back. Duke rose slowly from his desk. Bucky Minden looked up from a pile of papers and pushed his glasses back on his nose. He was the greenest on the force, so he worked with me most days.

Bucky was a good kid, but wouldn't last in law enforcement. He was a book smart guy with a sharp brain, but nerves like tinsel. Police work, even in a tiny pimple of a town like Luther's Bend wasn't the job for him. I always hoped he would discover that on his own.

They came at me with questions, and I did what I could to fill in the gaps. Bucky winced when I described the condition of Arthur Milton's body. "Totally F-ed up," Duke said with excitement, sounding like I'd just described a particularly spectacular event at a monster truck rally. Bucky just looked worried and uncomfortable. When I told them about the perp, their eyes grew narrow with suspicion. I even caught them exchanging a look.

"A mask?" Duke said. "How'd he eat up Arthur wearing a mask?"

"That's what the state boys are trying to figure out. For now, I want you two to get on the phones and let folks know that we have a curfew in place. No one under eighteen is to be out past sunset. Call the schools and have Janey post it to our website."

"You said his head looked like a dog or a wolf?" Bucky asked.

"Not his head, the mask," I corrected.

"Could it have been a jackal?" he asked.

"Bucky, I don't even know what a jackal looks like."

"It looks like a dog."

"Wouldn't that be covered by me saying the mask looked like a dog?"

Duke made a snorting sound and slapped Bucky's shoulder playfully. "Go ahead and ask another, Einstein. It's not like Bill has anything else to do this morning."

"Sorry," Bucky said. "The description just reminded me of something."

I must have been punch drunk with exhaustion because I almost let that comment slide, almost dismissed Bucky to get back to his desk and start the phone calls. I was even walking past him, headed for my office, ready to start in on my report. I didn't stop until I reached the threshold. Only then did I focus in on the fact that I was in the middle of a murder investigation. If Bucky had information that might move the investigation along for the state boys, I had to hear him out.

"Well, you said his body looked human," Bucky said nervously. He sat in a chair on the other side of my desk, fidgeting with the bow of his glasses. "And the head was canine. One of the primary figures of Egyptian mythology fits that description. They called him Anubis. He was a god of death or something. I don't remember exactly."

And there I was thinking that Bob had been nuts for saying *werewolf*. Now one of my own deputies was saying we had an Egyptian god in our little community.

It turns out that wasn't exactly what he was saying.

"People obsess on a lot of different things, Bill," Bucky continued. "Maybe our guy is obsessed with Egyptology or something, might belong to some kind of cult. His costume might actually be integral to his psychology. I don't know. It's just that your description got me to thinking."

"You got a picture of this Anubis?"

"They'll have pictures on the Internet," he said. "Just Google the name and hit the image tab."

And there it was. Sort of. It wasn't exactly what I'd seen, but it was damned close. The muzzle in the pictures was longer and thinner than the one I'd seen on the perp. The ears on Arthur's killer weren't as pronounced as those on the image, which stood high and pointed above the head. In fact, I don't even remember clearly what his ears had looked like, but the general features of a snout and the heavy brow and the muscular body were similar. All of the images that appeared showed this Anubis thing as being black, so the color was also wrong, but the overall impression was the same.

The likelihood that some insane mummy cult prowled Luther's Bend was a stretch to say the least. I was way too tired to realize exactly how silly it sounded, so I figured it was a viable avenue of investigation: no more ridiculous than looking for the Wolfman.

"You might have something," I told Bucky. His eyes lit up like a kid seeing a new bicycle. "Do some research. Put your thoughts together. We'll talk about it later."

Pleased and excited with the assignment, Bucky hurried from my office. Duke offered to stay on for a few more hours so I could rest, and I took him up on it. I wanted to see my kids. I was at the end of the longest day of my life and all I wanted was to have it over with.

"I'm sorry," Lisa said when I walked through the door. She wrapped her arms around my neck and held me close. "I'm so sorry. I wasn't thinking straight last night. You know what my migraines do to me."

"It's okay," I told her.

I was in no mood to get into the whole "migraine" argument. (I didn't know a single doctor that would prescribe vodka and Xanax as a migraine treatment, but I kept my mouth shut on the subject.) My head was full of bad thoughts, terrible images. All I wanted was to crawl into bed and hope to sleep through the worst of the nightmares I knew were waiting for me.

"Did Duke call you?"

"No, I saw it on the news. You looked just awful."

I was on the news? I didn't remember seeing cameras; I certainly didn't speak to any reporters.

"They were interviewing one of the state troopers, and I saw you come out of the woods over to the park."

"You heard about Arthur?"

"Yes," Lisa said. "God, I couldn't believe it. But Maggie is safe. That's something."

"I should call Les Mayflower."

"He already called to thank you. He's going to be home with Maggie and Vivian for the day. He said it might be better if you called his cell, though. A lot of people were trying to get through."

I knew that was right. When a crisis came down, the lines between friends and family blurred, and the good folks that knew Les, whether related by blood or not, would be offering any help they could.

"How are the girls?"

"They're fine. Still in bed."

It was after eight in the morning. Usually, Gwen and Dru were already in high gear by then. "At this hour?"

"I gave them something to help them sleep. They were so upset about little Maggie."

The term, "I saw red," suddenly made a lot of sense to me. Lisa, standing only a foot away from me, twinkled out of focus, blurred at the edges to a soft pink as the booming of my heart climbed my neck to nest at my temples. My entire body trembled.

"You what?"

"Just an Ambien. I split it in half for them."

"You gave our daughters sleeping pills?"

"Well would you rather they were up all night crying?" Lisa asked, her voice rising to the argument.

"Jesus Christ, Lisa, if you want to fuck up your own head, then by all means carry on, but you will not teach our children to hide their problems under prescriptions. What the hell were you thinking?"

"I *thought* I was helping."

"Helping?"

"Fine, Bill. Whatever. I poisoned them, okay? I'm a terrible mother and a horrible wife."

"Not this again."

"Everything I do is wrong."

"You drugged our kids, Lisa. Maybe if you weren't so wrapped up in your own shit, you'd see how completely fucked up that is. They are children, Lisa. Do you get that? Do you get that they are going to have problems and disappointments, and they are going to be scared, and they have to learn to deal with those things? If they don't, they're going to end up…"

Yes, the end of that sentence was *like you*. But I couldn't bring myself to say it. With all of the problems we'd endured over the last few years, it didn't need to be said. It was an avenue of argument we'd been up and down too many times.

Lisa was already walking away. She threw open the door to the coat closet, grabbed her jacket and headed for the front door.

"I have to be back to work in a few hours," I called.

The door slammed in reply.

The problems between us weren't new. The last few years had seen Lisa drifting further away from our daughters and me; drinking more, getting prescriptions for god knows what from Doctor Laughlin out at the clinic. She used to drink a glass of wine in the evening once the girls were put to bed. I didn't think anything about it. Hell, I'd go through a few beers a night myself. At some point, she replaced her glass of wine with a glass of vodka. It was a straight shot downhill from there.

Back then I traveled some. Actually, I traveled quite a bit, I suppose. I'd take off for a weekend of fishing or hunting, or go on up to Marrenville for a seminar on law enforcement. At least one weekend a month I kissed Lisa and the girls goodbye, climbed in my car and hit the road.

Lisa didn't let me know my travel upset her until it got to the point she was fed up with it. Maybe I was just too dense to notice subtle hints, if she had indeed given me any. I'm not certain. I was just back from a fishing trip with Les Mayflower, hadn't even stored my tackle box yet, and she met me in the garage with a scowl. She clutched a glass of vodka in one hand, the knuckles white from strain.

"Your daughter nearly got run down by a truck," Lisa said, her voice wavering with barely restrained fury.

The news startled me so badly I dropped my tackle box. "Is she okay? What happened?"

"Dru was playing in the street, not watching what she was doing, as usual, and that Colton kid with the Dodge came tearing down the road."

"Weren't you watching her?" I asked.

"I can't do everything, Bill! Gwen needed my help with her homework and Dru wanted to play. What was I supposed to do? I told her stay out of the road, but she's a child, and she doesn't listen. They never listen, and you're never around. You're out in the woods with Les, or over to his shop playing poker with those rednecks from Lowrey, or up in Marrenville with your cop buddies. Did you ever think that I might like a weekend in the city?"

"I go there for work," I said as my only defense.

"Well, good for you. You have work. I've been working every minute of every day since Gwen was born. Maybe I'd like to get away, do some shopping, have someone else fix a meal for a change."

Even as the tirade progressed, I was aware of the fact that nothing more was said about Dru or the truck that nearly ran her down, which led me to believe that Lisa was exaggerating the severity of the incident. Still, that didn't change the underlying message she delivered: *You're a bad husband and a bad father.* That message came through as clear as a pistol report on a mountaintop.

Guilt hit me pretty hard. Her attack was wholly unexpected and completely devastating. My gut was hollowed out, my head buzzing. Up until that point, I thought our life together was a good one, stable and secure and comfortable the way a family was supposed to be. Growing up, I watched my father pack his tackle box or his shotgun nearly every weekend. Weeknights he got together with his cronies at the barbershop, played cards or checkers, drank beer, until it was time to come home for some sleep. My mother never complained, never once looked out of sorts about it.

This life was what I knew; it never occurred to me that it might somehow be wrong.

But there was the gnawing, burrowing guilt, which to me was as good as an axe when it came to hobbling a guy.

So, I made a promise to Lisa. I promised to spend more time with her and with the girls. And that's exactly what I did.

My being around the house didn't help. If anything, it just made things worse. Lisa's migraines started a couple of months later. She took pills and drank herself through the sickness. At first, I was understanding and doted on her. I made dinner when I got home from the station, helped the girls with their homework, spent weekends playing with them in the park. I did what I could and didn't resent a single moment of it.

But Lisa kept on drifting, or maybe she was drowning. Whatever the case, I tried. It only drove her further away.

Upstairs, I checked on Gwen and Dru. They looked so peaceful, so beautiful. Obviously our argument had not disturbed them, and for that I was grateful. I kissed them both on the forehead, felt their breath on my chin.

I started to cry. Frustration. Relief. Fear. It all poured out of me, and I left the room so my sobs would not wake them.

TORN

After a quick shower, I climbed into bed. Though the idea of sleep seemed impossible, I drifted off immediately, and the nightmares I expected never came.

3

I drove to the station under a sky of angry clouds. Their gray cast reminded me of the man I'd seen the night before, the color of his skin. More than twelve hours had passed since seeing that freak hunched over Arthur with a good chunk of the man in his mouth, but already my mind was rearranging things. After all, I'd come upon that scene quickly. My lantern had cast such a harsh beam that his features and subtleties were bound to wash out. There had been no muzzle, I told myself, no pronounced brow. Some of those body builder types had strange looking faces; it was a side effect of all the steroids they pumped into their bodies. It sank their cheeks, tightened their skin so that it stretched over the bone in a wholly unnatural way. I'd seen it plenty of times in workout magazines back when I was trying to figure out exactly what all of those machines at City Fitness were for.

If I had seen anything resembling a muzzle it was a mask, as I'd first suspected.

And what if Emily Salem's description was accurate and we had a second crazy running around Luther's Bend? I'd have to get a better description from Emily and shoot that out over the wires, maybe hold a town meeting to instruct parents and their children about protecting themselves from sexual predators.

There was a lot of work waiting for me. I'd have preferred to be at home watching *Spongebob Squarepants* with my girls, listening to Dru's laughter and Gwen's shrill and excited impersonations of the boxy yellow character.

A news van sat parked in the lot at the station house. I felt a sudden vice of nerves squeezing my belly when I saw it. I didn't want to talk to the press. Anytime there had been trouble in the past, the state boys had handled it. If it wasn't big enough for them, then it wasn't big enough for the news.

I drove on past. At the next intersection, I made a U-turn and pulled my car to the curb. I called Les Mayflower, keeping my eye on the side of the station house. The blandness of the structure hit me then. It was a single story box made from sand-colored bricks, broken only by small rectangular windows. The frosted glass, reinforced by a mesh of wires, provided extra light for the holding cells. As I considered the dull manufacture of the building, a shadow moved across the pane of the first cell, and my heart beat faster. More action from the night before? Or was Duke giving a guided tour to the press? Either way, just seeing the movement disturbed me.

"Hey Bill," Les said. He sounded as exhausted as I felt.

"How are you holding up?" I asked. "Is Maggie okay?"

"She…uhm…she's fine. I mean, physically. He didn't… well…there were no signs of…"

His daughter hadn't been sexually assaulted. My head grew light with relief.

"She's still pretty shaken up, and her wrists are a bit raw from those ropes, but we're all praying and thanking God. It could have been…well…we're grateful things turned out the way they did."

"So am I," I said, not including my feeling about Arthur Milton's brutal murder. "And what about you? Are you okay?"

"Not so much," Les said. "This whole thing has got me to thinking…you know…about my life, about life in general, I guess. I need to change some things."

The way he said that agitated my nerves further. He was very upset, and with good reason, but I felt like he was about to make some great proclamation. I wasn't sure what that would mean, and he wasn't ready to tell me.

"Look," he said. "We'll talk later. I'm trying to head neighbors off before they get to the door. Everybody is being so wonderful, but Maggie needs her rest. So, let's talk later."

"We'll have lunch in a couple of days, once things have calmed down a little."

"Sure," Les said, sounding distracted and uneasy. "You better let me go. The Salems are coming up the walk."

"Take care of yourself, Les."

I rang off and stared at the back of the station house, dread seeping through me like cold sludge. Too many things were going to change, I felt that.

Maybe it was time for a change, but *I* wasn't ready for it.

I walked into a nest of activity. Half a dozen strangers gathered in the main room. Duke was speaking quietly to three of them, while the other three looked around as if bored.

"Here he is," Duke said when he saw me.

Suddenly, all six of the strangers were coming at me like starving bums chasing down a donut. One of the men hoisted a camera to his shoulder and hustled around the reception counter. A light popped in my eyes. Voices swooped at me like birds.

Questions came in a torrent, babbled with such speed and volume that the actual queries were lost amid the noise. They called my name—*Sheriff Cranston...Sheriff Cranston...*—as if I was standing across the street and not inches from them. It was the only thing I made out initially because the rest got lost in that flood.

"Hold on," I said. "Who are you people?"

"Have you identified the suspect?" a handsome young man with bleached hair and a deep tan asked. The question set off another chorus of demands from the others. The blond guy, insisting to be heard, shouted, "Do you believe you've captured the man responsible for the murder of Arthur Milton?"

"They're from the press," Duke shouted over the crowd. "Can't you tell by them curved beaks?"

None of the faces belonged to employees of our local paper. Journalists from the city? I had to be impressed with the determination it had taken for them to make it down to Luther's Bend so quickly, but I still wasn't ready to deal with their questions, especially since I wasn't sure what they were talking about.

"Well then," I said, eyeing a particularly frantic looking little man with a sweaty bald head, "I guess I'm going to have to ask you to wait outside for a few minutes."

None of the crowd seemed happy about this. I pushed through them, shot Duke an angry look and continued toward my office.

"You heard the man," Duke called. "Take it outside. We have some official business to take care of."

In my office, I dropped down into my chair. As if I didn't have enough to worry about, now the press wanted a statement. I didn't know what to tell them. While I sat there, trying to put together an intelligent sentence, something one of the reporters said crowded into my head.

Do you believe you've captured the man responsible for the murder of Arthur Milton?

A strange thing to ask. We hadn't caught anyone, as far as I knew. If the state boys had a suspect, they hadn't thought to let me know. It was a confusing question; one that was cleared up a few minutes later when Duke told me about the man in our holding cell.

"Why the hell didn't you call me?"

Duke's long face went crimson. I could see the wheels turning beneath his buzz cut, trying to come up with an acceptable excuse. "You were exhausted. We had it under control."

I leapt out of my chair and walked for the door. "If you have a suspect in custody, you call me. Okay? Jesus Christ, where did you pick him up?"

"Bucky was out patrolling the park this morning. He apprehended the guy trying to break into a car."

We passed through the main office, and I paused at the door to the holding cells, feeling around my belt for the keys.

"How long has he been here?"

"About an hour."

"Jesus Christ, Duke. You had me walking into an ambush back there. Why the hell did the press know about this before I did?"

"I don't know," Duke said. "But we got the asshole. I mean, one of them anyway. The guy matches Emily Salem's description to a T."

"So do a lot of people," I reminded him, finally finding the right key and slotting it into the lock.

"Yeah, I know," Duke said. "But most of them aren't trying to break into cars bare-ass naked."

Duke's last comment made me pause. Naked? Where the hell had the man been all night that no one had spotted him?

Dismayed by yet another oddity to add to the list, I told Duke to go handle the press. "Tell them we have a suspect in the Salem case. That's all we know right now. Did you question him?"

"Tried. He wouldn't say a thing. Just stares at the floor."

"You got a name on this guy?" I asked.

"Well, the car he was trying to break into was a rental. It was taken out yesterday by a guy named Sykes. Douglas Sykes. We popped the lock and found the rental papers and his wallet in the glove box. The name's good."

With Duke on my heels, I opened the door and stepped into the dimly lit hallway. Douglas Sykes sat on the cot in the first of four holding cells. The window above, barred and frosted, allowed only a meager bath of natural light. The fixture in the ceiling held a low watt bulb. Even taking these things into account, I thought the holding area looked particularly dark. The suspect was wrapped in one of the gray blankets we used to make up the cots. He sat with his back propped on the cinderblock wall. His hair was thin and white, long wisps jutting from his head like tangled spider silk. A high forehead banked down to bushy black eyebrows. He had brown, rather bland eyes, a sharp nose and narrow lips, at the moment drawing a straight line across his face, revealing no discernible emotion. With no concession to modesty, the blanket ran off to the sides, revealing a narrow, sunken chest, a wild nest of white pubic hair that all but hid his penis, and two stick thin legs, bent at the knee with the soles of his feet planted firmly on the cot.

In most regards, he looked like an old man who couldn't be bothered to take care of himself. Though he certainly fit the description Emily Salem had given of Maggie Mayflower's abductor, he was not the man I'd seen carrying Arthur Milton through the forest like a sack of feathers. His face was cruel looking, but sometimes that was simply a side effect of age and gravity. The only thing remarkable about his appearance was his skin. It was powder white and hung off his bones, loose and draping as if he'd recently lost about a hundred pounds.

"Why isn't this man dressed?" I asked.

"Bill, I told you, this is how we found him."

"Get him some clothes, Officer Gill. And then go make that statement to the press."

I noticed through this exchange that Sykes did not look up, nor did he seem particularly interested in our being there. He stared forward at the space between his feet.

"Mr. Sykes," I said, once Duke was moving toward the door. "Mr. Sykes, I'm Sheriff Cranston."

Behind me, Duke walked through the door and closed it. I heard the crack of the lock being secured. Good. The idiot was finally doing his job.

"Mr. Sykes…"

But I didn't have a chance to finish. The man on the cot lifted his head, and his thin lips shot up into a crazy grin. His eyes, the ones I'd thought so bland, ignited with excitement. He did not leave his place on the cot, but suddenly the whole scene seemed different.

"Bill," he said, like he was welcoming an old friend. "We don't have much time, you know. No. No. Not much time to show or blow; for soon, so soon, I must go."

"Mr. Sykes, do you understand why you're being held?"

"Not much time you and I; time is an insect, time is a fly."

Nut case. His singsong rhymes, delivered in a deep throaty tone too rich for his fragile appearance, made the diagnosis easy enough. This naked as a jaybird poet was off his fucking rocker.

"Mr Sykes, we're going to hold you until the state troopers can transfer you to the facility in Marrenville. Until then, if you have anything you'd like to talk about, perhaps regarding a little girl, I'm all ears."

"Sweet, sweet Maggie," said Sykes.

I was glad to see that he could respond without a couplet, and I was also pleased to have what I considered a partial confession.

"Maybe you'd like to tell me what happened last night?"

"By the park; before dark?"

"Would you mind confirming for me that your name is Douglas Sykes?"

"That is me; and I am he."

"And you admit to having abducted Maggie Mayflower at approximately six p.m.?"

"She took my hand," Sykes said in his gruff yet melodic voice. "We walked the land."

"And what was your intent, Mr. Sykes?"

Behind me, the lock cracked, announcing Duke's return. The officer entered the holding area, carrying a stack of clothes.

"I found what I could in the lockers. It ain't fashion, but it'll work."

I took the clothes from Duke and turned to the prisoner.

Douglas Sykes stared at the space between his feet. His expression blank. Apparently, I was the only one he felt like performing for. I tossed garments through the bars, did a good job of making them land on the cot, though a balled pair of socks clipped Sykes's shin and rolled onto the concrete floor.

I told Duke to take care of those reporters and to send Bucky in with the digital camera. Though it wouldn't be considered official, I wanted both Maggie and Emily Salem to give this guy a look so we had a positive identification, though I in no way wanted them in this holding area with him. The state boys would do the ID official and proper, but this was for my own piece of mind and that of the community. Folks like Les needed to know we had at least one of the right freaks behind bars.

Again, once the lock was engaged, Sykes came to life.

"You have til sunset, Bill."

"Really? And what happens at sunset?"

"Such wonders and blunders sunset brings."

"Well, Mr. Sykes, by sunset you'll be up to Marrenville in a county lockup with about twenty other men, none of whom take kindly to pedophiles."

"I don't think I will… Bill."

"We'll have to agree to disagree on that one. You feel like telling me what you're doing in my town?"

"Away from those who know me; eyes that pry but don't see." Sykes smile faded and he fixed a nasty gaze on me, full of accusation and anger. "You know what I mean don't you, Bill? Someplace far from home where our precious filthy secrets can be indulged, but not revealed?"

I grew uncomfortable at Sykes's remarks. I didn't know this man, and he certainly didn't know me, yet for some reason, he felt compelled to draw a comparison between us. I'd heard that some psychos could get into your head, draw out information to use against you. It was like those TV psychics who dropped vague hints until they hit on something relevant to one of the suckers in the audience, and then they worked that scrap of knowledge into the shape of revelation.

It was a cute game. But I wasn't going to play.

"Why don't you put some clothes on now," I said. "I'll be back in to chat with you before the state boys show up."

With that, Sykes rolled off the cot and let the blanket fall to the concrete, where it pooled at his feet. His body was disgusting. The skin looked as if it was separated from the muscle beneath, wanting nothing to do with him. Tufts of thin white hair grew at his shoulders. Pink lines, like scars, ran over his arms, his chest, his belly. They looked like the stretch marks Lisa had worn after giving birth to Gwen. But something else on his shoulder drew my attention.

Just below where the collarbone peaked, Sykes wore a brown scab the size of a nickel. My eyes immediately traced down the grotesque body, past a nest of moles on his lower abdomen, over his pubic region and to his thigh where I found a second scab, identical to the first.

The wounds unnerved me. I'd felt certain that I'd shot a far larger man, a man in a mask, in those exact places the night before.

I backed away, suddenly feeling a need to be out of this space and away from Douglas Sykes. His voice crawled over my shoulder when I reached the door, but I didn't turn back.

"You have til sunset."

I drove toward the Mayflower home. The digital camera sat on the seat next to me. During the drive, I was struck time and again by my inability to accept what I had seen on Sykes's body. Those scabs were in nearly the exact locations of the bullet wounds I'd inflicted on another man the night before. But that man was huge and powerful with skin the color of old beef and teeth sharp enough to rip the muscle from Arthur Milton's bones.

Werewolf, Bob Dawson said.

And whenever that memory, that word, came to me, I felt foolish and childish, refuting such nonsense outright. Bucky's supposition about an Egyptian myth was even more ridiculous. Those wounds on Sykes could have been anything. They were already well into healing. He could have jabbed himself on a branch, could have had a couple of his moles removed, could have been running with scissors for all I knew. As for the appearance of his skin, sagging and lifeless as if recently stolen from a large corpse, Sykes was old, and some old people just looked like crap. It wasn't their fault; that was their prize for living so long.

By the time I reached the Mayflower driveway, my thoughts were tied up as tight as wet twine.

I decided to speak with Les's neighbor first. After all, Emily, too, had been a witness. I didn't want to put Les and his family through any more than I had to. If Emily gave me a positive ID then I'd confirm it with Maggie, if not I'd let it drop until the state boys got around to Sykes. I walked across the street and knocked on the Salems' door.

When Emily Salem saw the digital picture of Douglas Sykes, her face went pale, and she clutched at her father's leg. Dick Salem asked to see the man and made a gruff snort when I showed him the image on the screen.

"Any chance you'd give me ten minutes alone in that cell with the bastard?" he asked.

"Afraid not."

I knelt down and looked in Emily's eyes, saw the fear there. "Now, honey, are you certain this is the man you saw with Maggie?"

The little girl nodded her head furiously and then snuggled deeper into her father's pant leg.

Dick walked me out to the porch. He told me that Emily was feeling better, had actually spoken a bit over breakfast. He imagined she'd be just fine in a week or two once the initial fear was good and worn. He thanked me for my efforts, shook my hand and walked back into his house.

At the Mayflower's home, Les answered the door, looking uneasy. I couldn't blame him. I'd called ahead to let him know why I was coming by. No parent wanted to put their child through this kind of misery; I certainly wouldn't have wanted Gwen or Dru to endure it. Les was so upset, he barely looked at me. Didn't shake my hand. He just opened the door and stepped back.

"Mag and Viv are upstairs," he said. "First door on the left."

I reached out to give his shoulder a supportive squeeze, but Les backed away. His burly body all but leapt away from my touch. His thick fingers combed through the salt and pepper hair on his crown, and he looked at the floor.

I thought I understood, but Les said something that made me think I was wrong.

"We're being punished, aren't we?" he asked. "I mean, by God."

"What?"

Les wasn't a religious guy, no more so than myself at any rate. He went to church, had a bible on his bookcase that he never read. He took his family to the church socials, the potluck picnics. That's why his words struck me so wrong; they sounded like the claims of a burgeoning fanatic.

"That guy could have taken Emily Salem, but he didn't. He took my little girl. He took Maggie. It's got to mean something."

"It means a sick bastard came to town. Jesus, Les. This isn't some divine retribution. God has nothing to do with this guy. That much I know."

But Les didn't look up. He stared at the floor, shame faced and near tears.

"Bill…" Les said, shaking his head.

"You can't take the blame for this. You'll drive yourself crazy with it. Now, I'll only be upstairs for a couple of minutes. You wait here."

I left Les at the bottom of the stairs. Viv gave me a tight hug when I walked into Maggie's room. She was a good-looking woman, if a bit thick around the middle. In fact she and Les shared a similar build, though where her husband had muscle Viv carried less firm weight. Her face was lovely though. Tears had reddened and swollen her eyes, but that only made her look more attractive, something about the vulnerability.

Across the room, Maggie sat on the edge of her bed, watching us. She was wearing white pajamas with a teddy bear print on them, and her hair was pulled back into a bushy pony tail.

"Hey Maggie," I said, separating myself from Viv's tight embrace. "How are you feeling?"

"I'm fine, Officer Cranston," she replied in a sweet, albeit dry, voice. The child climbed off of her bed and walked cautiously toward me. She seemed okay except for the bandages around her wrists. I'm sure she wasn't okay though. How could she be?

"I want you to look at something," I said.

"We told her why you were coming over," Viv whispered.

I called up the picture on the digital camera, and when I had it on the screen, I leaned down and held it at Maggie's eye level. "Now, is this the man that took you into the woods?"

Maggie looked at the picture of Douglas Sykes. A series of emotions ran over her face, her features changing from one second to the next as if stricken by tics. Finally she backed away from the screen, nodding her head.

"Is that the man, Maggie? Is this what he looked like?"

"Yes," the little girl said, walking back to her bed. "At first."

"What do you mean, at first?"

"He changed," Maggie said.

The little girl's voice chilled me then. My skin pimpled under my shirt, drew tight over my back and shoulders.

"How did he change, Maggie?"

"He got bigger," she said. "Then, he ran away and hid, right up to the time Mr. Milton found me. When he came back, he was a monster."

"She's very confused," Viv whispered over my shoulder. "The doctor said that she might have trouble remembering things. Blocking it all out, getting things mixed up."

But Maggie wasn't confused. A strange acceptance settled on me then. Despite ridiculing all that I thought true in life, I found myself believing the little girl. Maggie knew what she had seen and wasn't burdened with all of the mature filters she needed to deny it. She remembered seeing Sykes turn into a monster, because that's exactly what he had done.

4

"What did you mean when you said I had until sunset?"

"Wouldn't it be swell; if I were to tell?"

He sat on the cot in the same position I'd found him in that morning. He was dressed in the clothes Duke had scrounged from the lockers: a pair of blue jeans that pooled around his waist but rode up high on his shins; a baggy white T-shirt and socks. The excited expression was on his face again.

Unease ran over my skin. I looked away, down the alley of the holding area past the two empty cells. Nothing around me but concrete and metal, and the prisoner behind the wall of bars, but it felt like the room teamed with less corporeal beings, jostling and shoving, groping at me as they floated through the narrow hall. I attributed much of my disquiet to the conversation I'd had with Maggie Mayflower. She'd seen this man change, and I'd seen what he had become—Arthur Milton's brutal assailant—but I had no idea what such a creature was capable of.

"What are you, Sykes?"

"Just a man, like Stan or Dan." His eyes twinkled with mischief, exposing the lie.

"But you're not," I said. "You're something else."

"Am I?" He asked in mock surprise. Then his face fell into an expression of boredom or contempt. "Do a blood test, Bill. Take a tissue sample. See what modern science makes of me. It won't be very interesting, I'm afraid. If you were to put a bullet through my head right now; they'd find absolutely nothing unique in the autopsy."

"You shouldn't put those kinds of ideas in my head."

"But I *want* them in your head, Bill."

The unnerving parade of spirits pushed in tight to my back, tickled my neck. Something about Sykes's voice and manner. More craziness, I thought. Some new insanity to throw me off when I needed real information. "Did you attack Arthur Milton last night?"

"Was that the name of the man with the enormous shlong?"

"Someone murdered Arthur last night. Was it you?"

Sykes laughed. He dropped his head back and let it roll against the cinderblock.

"There once was a man from Nantucket…"

"Sykes!"

"What did you think of that, Bill? That cock, I mean. It was pretty damned impressive. I'll bet someone is weeping over its loss. Some poor woman…or man. That's going to leave a tremendous void."

"Did you murder Arthur Milton?"

"Bill," Sykes said, his voice sharp and edged with anger. "You saw what killed him. Now, did it look like me?"

"No."

"Then why ask?" Sykes's eyes sparkled at that question. "It's my job."

"It's your job to ask ridiculous questions? What does a position like that pay?"

"Are you saying there was someone else? Another man?"

The discomfort with Sykes was deep into my nerves now; the sense of something ominous sharing the room was overpowering. I wanted out of the holding area, wanted to be away from Sykes, with several locked doors between us, but there was more I needed to know.

"Is he coming back tonight?" I asked.

"He's not the one you should be worried about, Bill."

"Then why don't you tell me what I should be worried about?"

"Wouldn't it be swell; if I were to tell?"

"Fine," I said, standing from the chair. "Sit here until the state boys show. You can entertain them with your fairy rhymes."

"What an unenlightened comment."

"Fuck you, Sykes," I said.

"Tell me something, Bill," Sykes said, causing me to pause at the door. "Does your wife know?"

Infuriated with Sykes's games, I stormed into the office, startling Bucky Minden into dropping a pile of papers.

"I don't want anyone going in there," I told him. "When will the troopers be around for him?"

Bucky, still looking flustered, pushed his glasses back up on his nose. "I was just going to tell you. They have themselves a situation at the rest area off exit twenty-seven."

I knew the place. It was only six miles up the interstate. "What happened?"

"They aren't sure," Bucky said. "They found some abandoned vehicles… a couple of semis and an SUV. Windows were broken out. They found some blood at the scene, but no bodies. They're doing a sweep of the area now."

I considered Douglas Sykes, then. He'd had a lot of time between Arthur's murder and his arrest early that morning. The rest area in question sat on the northern edge of the forest. He could have made it there and back with time to spare. "Do they think it's connected to Arthur's attack?"

"Couldn't say, Sheriff."

"Well, I don't want this freak here overnight."

"Yes, Sir," Bucky said, looking frightened, as if I'd asked him to take Sykes home and put him up in a guest room.

I slammed the door to my office and dropped into my chair. What the hell had Sykes meant about Lisa? What was she supposed to know? Hell, she wasn't conscious enough throughout the course of the day to know much of anything, but what exactly was the prisoner asking?

We're being punished, Les said.

An uneasy flush rose in my cheeks.

I chatted with State Trooper Coltraine at three that afternoon. His voice carried a tone of calm efficiency, though I could tell he was feeling a bit rattled about the night's events. In addition to Arthur's murder, they were now burdened by the rest area mystery. According to Coltraine, a salesman by the name of Tubbs drove into the rest area at just after five that morning, trying to make it up to Marrenville for an eight a.m. meeting. When he arrived, he noticed the SUV, its passenger-side windows smashed, glass all over the concrete. He called the troopers, and they came on the scene to find two semi cabs similarly beat up. No signs of the drivers. They had already done a thorough search of the buildings ("found some blood in the men's room") and the fields spreading out to the East ("didn't find a damned thing"). They were going into the woods about the time Coltraine called me.

As for Sykes, Coltraine said, "We still have men in your area, following up on last night. I'm surprised they haven't checked in with you yet. At any rate, they have instructions to pick Sykes up on their way back. I'm sure they'll be along shortly."

I ended the call, then dialed my house. I told Lisa I'd be working late, and she hung up on me.

Since Sykes was going to be with us longer than I'd thought or wanted, I sent Bucky on down to Peg's Diner to get our prisoner some food. While he was gone, I went back into the holding area, took my chair.

"It's almost sunset," Sykes said, his gaze rising to the ceiling. "Time's almost up."

"Time for what?"

"For Bill; to kill." Sykes smiled and aimed his index finger at me, cocked his thumb. "Bang. Bang."

"Who am I going to kill?"

"Obviously; it is me."

"You want me to kill you?"

"Not especially. But I think it's time."

"And why's that?"

"The fun is done; old and tired; and just can't run."

"Well, I hate to disappoint you."

"No disappointment," Sykes said. He threw his legs over the edge of the cot and stood. "It'll happen with or without you. They'll tear me to shreds."

"And who are *they*?" I backed my chair closer to the wall behind me.

"Wouldn't it be swell; if I were to tell?"

"Where did you go after you killed Arthur last night?"

"Have I confessed to anything? I think not."

"Where did you go?"

"Into the woods," said Sykes, "where all fairy tales live."

"North? South? What direction?"

"Couldn't say, Bill. When you're scared, your only interest is speed and distance."

"So you were scared by something?"

Sykes snorted a laugh and leaned his face against the bars. "Certainly not by you."

"I don't think you were scared at all. I'm thinking you headed north and found yourself a few more victims."

"How seedy; how greedy. I'm neither seedy nor greedy."

The man was infuriating, but that was his intent. He wanted to throw me off balance and keep me there with his ridiculous poetry and his cryptic phrases, using verbal craziness to keep from providing any real information. I doubted I could match him with sheer creativity, but I thought about something Bucky had said and decided to throw a curveball of my own.

"Tell me about Anubis," I said.

But Sykes wasn't fazed. His smile never faltered; he didn't bat an eye.

"Just another beast mistaken for a God," he said. "They couldn't comprehend, much like you, so they demonized and deified, offering up sacrifices to keep the beast from the threshold so they could sleep a little easier."

"You don't think he's worth worshipping?"

"Bill, you're too concerned with the past. You should be concentrating on the present, because it's far less comforting. Your friends, your family, they can't be harmed by dust and history. But they can be harmed."

"Are you threatening my family?"

"A perfect life. A lovely wife," Sykes sang. He spun away from the bars in a graceful series of steps that took him to the center of the room. "It must be nice, this perfect life."

"Sykes!"

"I had a beautiful wife," he said, returning to the cell door. "Her name was Lolita, just like Nabokov's darling bitch, and she was a seductress, she was. Oh, she did take my tongue on trips. I provided well and was attentive, was a model husband, if I do say so myself. But I had to leave home several times a month, you see. I had issues of my own. Secrets. I'm sure *you* understand. I always wondered why my Lolita didn't accept my excuses. They were well thought out, confirmed as well as any truth could be confirmed. She never discovered anything. Not one iota of proof. But she knew. Oh yes, she did. She smelled the deceit on me."

"And you think this story applies to me?"

Sykes lowered his head, brow pressed to the bars. "Don't you, Bill?"

"No, Sykes, I really don't."

"Pity. A shitty pity."

"So your wife left you. You divorced."

This set Sykes to laughing. "No, Bill. We didn't divorce and she didn't leave; I tore her throat out with my teeth."

Unease returned like wind, whispering over the hairs on my neck. I trembled for a moment, tried to hide it, but it just got worse as I gazed on the amused prisoner facing me.

"Ready to kill me now?"

"No. But I think I'll get back to my desk." I stood from the chair and pushed it back against the wall. "Thank you."

"Oh, but there are so many more questions to ask," said Sykes.

I didn't know why he was trying to keep me in the holding area, didn't know what he hoped to accomplish by it, but he wasn't done talking yet.

"Don't you want to know why sweet Maggie wasn't injured?"

"I'm sure the state boys will supply me with a full report."

"Aren't you the least bit curious?"

"No, Sykes."

But he wasn't listening. Sykes seemed desperate for me to remain.

"Because even the beast has some humanity in him. Sometimes people get this idea that it's all or nothing. It's all man. Or, it's all monster. But that's not the case. The humanity is always there. And the beast is always there."

In the abstract, he was talking about compulsion. I'd read plenty about it when it came to sex offenders and serial killers. Though a completely human defect, compulsion didn't explain what I had seen the night before.

"You kidnapped a little girl and ate a grown man raw."

"It's the hate, Bill. The beast's absolute loathing for the species that harbors and subdues it is overpowering. It punishes and feeds; it tears and it bleeds."

"But we're not talking about an 'it;' we're talking about you."

"I am me. Can't you see? I am me and he is he. When he is he, I can't be me. I'd think you of all people would appreciate the distinction I was making."

"Really? Maybe I'm a bit dense."

"Maybe," Sykes agreed. "But I can still smell him on you, Bill."

I couldn't breathe, couldn't speak. I opened my mouth but nothing came out.

Then, Bucky pushed open the door, holding a Styrofoam container with a can of pop balanced on top of it. He looked at me, saw the expression I was wearing and concern spread over his face.

"Sheriff?" he asked.

"Leave the food and get out," I told him. "Don't disturb us unless the state boys show up."

"Yes, sir."

I looked at the prisoner, sitting so calmly on his cot, ignoring the chicken dinner I'd slid through the bars, though sipping occasionally from the can of pop. A dozen questions played bumper cars in my skull. Beneath his black eyebrows, his eyes were intense but no longer manic. This man admitted to savagely murdering his wife; this man said he used Maggie Mayflower as bait; this man said he knew a beast, but the beast was not him. On this last point, I believe I understood his cryptic claim. He was not claiming innocence, simply a lack of control.

"Is the beast coming back tonight?" I asked. "Is that why you said I had until sunset?"

"You wish it were that simple."

"Is it coming back?"

Sykes dropped the empty pop can on the concrete floor. He raised a fist and flipped out his fingers, counting while he said, "More than one, more than two; oh whatever, whatever will you do? I think it would be best for you to release me, though I doubt you would. Perhaps you should just shoot me, Bill. It'll save us both a lot of trouble. You could tell them I was trying to escape."

"I'm not the kind of man that shoots an unarmed prisoner."

"And what kind of *man* are you?"

"Leave me out of this," I shouted at the old man, still rubbed raw by his earlier comment. "I want to know more about your beast."

"Well, you met him last night. Handsome thing, isn't he?"

"You think he can get you out of that cage?"

"Bill, you're too worried about what can get out. Think about what can get in."

"Why don't you just tell me what can get in?"

"Oh, the angry ones, they're no fun. They want to kill, want to scar; because I made them what they are." Sykes' amused expression clouded. He leaned forward, resting his forearms on his knees and stared through the bars at me. "In short, Bill, you have a pack descending on this town. I imagine they're the ones who caused your troubles up north. So, here's what you do. You multiply the beast you saw last night by nine or ten. You take that well-hung Arthur I gnawed and put the faces of all your friends on that body, because that's what's going to be left of your little town."

"So, I'm supposed to just let you out of that cell, let you walk away to save my town from a pack of...what? Werewolves? That'll look good in the papers."

"There's always the bullet, Bill." Sykes leaned back against the wall, looked around the cell as he said, "I'd prefer that myself. They won't be so kind."

"Why do they want you?"

"Superstition. Ignorance. They saw a movie or read a book. They believe there's a curse they can end by ending me. They got themselves the flu, and they think killing the guy that gave it to them will stop their noses from running."

"And strangely enough, they choose now, when you're locked up, to make this attack. That's awfully convenient, Sykes."

"Not convenient at all." His voice was weary. He shook his head, slowly at first and then with great ferocity, unsettling his wispy hair. When he spoke again, some of his previous energy had returned. "I took great care to find hunting grounds for the beast far from my home, and I returned only rarely to the places I'd been before. When I kissed my wife goodbye, back when she still had lips, I took the beast into the world, following a calculated pattern of randomness. It is with great sadness that I realize my efforts became predictable. They anticipated this area."

"They'd make fine detectives, wouldn't they?" But even as I delivered that smart ass comment, I remembered the night before in the midnight woods, feeling that I was not only being stalked, but also surrounded. Thoughts about that rest area up north also creeped in.

"Oh, the mockery, the shockery," Sykes said. He climbed from the bed and approached the bars. "They are coming, Bill. They will follow my scent through the streets of your happy town, and they will eat themselves strong every step of the way."

Through the frosted glass above Sykes's head, I saw the dimming light. How long until sunset? An hour? Certainly no more than that.

As to whether I believed Sykes or not, I couldn't say. I felt a pressure on my back, no longer the subtle embrace of spirits, but a terrible burden that weighed like a wall I was trying to keep from tumbling down. He was insane, but that didn't make him wrong. At this same hour the day before, if anyone had suggested I'd be interrogating a monster, I would have laughed it off.

Truth is, what I was willing to believe had changed dramatically over the last twenty-four hours.

"If I were you," Sykes said. "I'd call your *friend*. His little girl is just swimming in my scent."

I didn't call Les, not at first. The first thing I did was walk into the station's main room and appraise the building. Brick construction: that was good. A solid door with metal reinforcement (glad I hadn't had the money to replace it with one of those glass ones I liked). But there was a long window across the front of the building. Another ran in the hallway leading to the lockers and the firing range to the back. My office was sealed up tight, as was the entire back of the building—only a fire door back there, which couldn't be opened from the outside.

The windows were the building's only weakness.

Bucky gave me a few curious looks, ducked his head back into the book he was reading.

"Any word from the state boys?" I asked. If those assholes would do their job, Sykes wouldn't be my problem any more, but my hope for them was already dried up.

"No, sir," he said. "Not a word since about three."

"Okay then, get Duke on the phone. I want him here now. The same goes for Ed."

"What's up, Sheriff?" Bucky asked, concern shading his brow.

"Call it a staff meeting."

In my office, I closed the door. While I was dialing the number to my house, my elbow clipped the stapler on my desk. I didn't even feel it, but I heard it clack on the linoleum, and my heart tripped like hail on a snare drum.

My eldest, Gwen, answered the phone. Her sweet and shy voice was barely audible.

"Hey, sweetheart, this is daddy."

"Hi, Daddy. When are you coming home?"

"Not for a while yet. Can you put your mother on the phone?"

"She's sick," Gwen said. "Her head hurts."

Son of a bitch. Two days in a row? My jangled nerves went raw, just plain burned with anger. Even if Gwen or Dru could manage to wake their mother, Lisa would be in no condition to drive. So, what was I supposed to do? Leave my kids alone in the house with their zoned out mother and hope that Sykes was truly delusional, or that the pack he mentioned would find no reason to go to my house. (Would Sykes's scent be on me? Even if it was, I hadn't been home since I'd found him incarcerated. Was I close enough to him last night to be tainted?) None of those questions mattered. My children were essentially alone and without defense. I couldn't just leave them there. Lisa either, for that matter.

"Sweetheart, I want you to do me a favor. I want you and your sister to put some clothes in your backpacks, just enough for a sleepover. Also, put some juice boxes and some of those snack bars in your lunch boxes."

"A sleepover?" Gwen chirped, very excited by the news. "Where?"

I didn't know. It didn't matter. I wanted my family out of town. With any luck, I could look back on this call and laugh at my foolishness.

"It's a surprise, sweetheart. Just tell your sister and try to wake your mother up."

5

Terrible thoughts rode with me across town. I called Les's house three times but only got the machine. I'd hoped to have Les pick up the girls and then make up an excuse for why his family and mine should be out of town for the night. I didn't have a clue what I would have said, but it didn't matter. The Mayflowers were not answering.

I wasn't prepared to believe the worst. It was not yet sunset, but it was coming fast. Les may have decided to take the family to his parents' place up north, just to get Maggie out of town for a couple of days, away from the memories of what Douglas Sykes had done to her. I tried his cell phone, but it went into his voice mail after the third ring. My thoughts being what they were, I imagined Les saw my name on the caller ID and turned the phone off. He'd said all he'd intended to say to me earlier and now wanted some peace with his family.

I left a message on his cell phone, demanding that he call me or meet me at the station. I had a big favor to ask. Since Lisa was likely to be in no condition to get my daughters out of town, my hope was to convince Les to do it. His family and mine needed to be far away from Luther's Bend before night fell; that was the only thing I could be certain of.

Instead of driving straight home, I made a detour, drove east until I picked up Whitehall Road. I wasn't sure what I expected to see in the park, but that was where all of the trouble had begun, where Douglas Sykes had snatched Maggie, and I imagined that if his pack did exist, they might just start where he'd started.

I slowed as I approached the playground area, noticing a family gathered on the deep sand amid the swingsets, the jungle gym and the tube-sprouting tree house. It occurred to me that they were just out for a picnic, though the weather seemed a bit cool for that. Two kids, an elderly woman that was probably their grandmother, and a rather odd grouping of adults, ranging from late twenties to middle-age, loitered there.

But as I approached them, every member of the family turned toward the car. Their manner of dress was incongruent, both with the weather and with each other. A slender man with a tattoo on his shoulder wore no shirt at all. He looked like he'd been plucked right out of the trailer park, dangling cigarette and mullet intact. I noticed with more than a little fear that his skin hung loose from his bones. Though the sagging flesh was not nearly so pronounced as it had been on Sykes, it was enough to send my heart into my throat. Next to the white trash guy stood a strikingly handsome man, perhaps a full decade older than I. The man wore his silver hair smoothed back. In his polo shirt and khaki slacks,

he looked like a bank executive on vacation. Even the two children came from different cultures. One was an Asian boy with short hair and tattered jeans. The other child, a girl, was much older, possibly Hispanic or Native American. She wore a very pretty blue summer dress and no shoes. Her left arm was missing below the elbow.

I drew closer and the old woman lifted her nose into the air as if taking a deep breath. Then she lowered her gaze and bared her teeth at me in a cruel grimace. The others wore disdain and anger. Only the older man, the one who looked like an executive, only his face didn't change. He was weighing the situation, mentally calculating some unknown equation; it burned like embers in his eyes.

Normally, I would have stopped and questioned strangers if they looked out of place in my town, or at the very least, given them a wave to let them know they were on my radar. Instead, I stepped on the gas and sped away.

My daughters met me at the door with hugs and kisses to my cheek. Both were wearing their Power Puff Girl backpacks, excited and eager to be going for a "surprise" sleepover. I held them close, smelling their hair, feeling their little hearts beating against me.

"Are you all ready?" I asked.

"Yes, Daddy," they said in unison.

"Good. Is your mother ready?"

Gwen's face grew serious and she shook her head. Dru's head fell, chin to chest.

"Mommy's asleep. She said she didn't want to go," Gwen said. "She said she wanted to be left alone."

I looked out the window, checked the day's darkening. There wasn't much time, but I couldn't just leave Lisa behind. Not now that I'd brought Sykes's scent into my home.

"Okay, young ladies," I said, manufacturing the biggest smile I could. "You two go get in the car, and you lock the doors. Mommy and daddy will be out in just a minute."

I watched them until they got to the car. Gwen helped her younger sister into the back seat before joining her there. Then she wriggled between the front seats and reached for the driver's side door. I saw the lock pin drop and disappear. Satisfied, I ran up the stairs and burst into the bedroom I shared with my wife.

Lisa bolted up in the bed, startled, looking around the room with her heavy-lidded gaze. Upon recognizing me, her face twisted sourly, and she dropped back to the pillow.

"Get up," I said, stomping across the room to the bed.

"Leave me alone. I have a migraine."

"Stop the shit, Lisa. This is serious."

"I'm sick."

"I don't doubt that, but we have got to leave, right now."

"Just go away and let me sleep."

"Lisa, I'm saying this once, and then I'm going to carry you out of here. The lunatic that killed Arthur is still out there, and now he's after me. That means he's after you and the girls too. So get your ass out of that bed and come on!"

It was a functional lie, certainly as close to the truth as I could get without having to spend thirty minutes defending my sanity. Still, it didn't work.

"Just go," she mumbled.

I reached down, intending to scoop her out of the bed. I'd carry her to the car if I had to. But Lisa rolled, throwing her elbow in the process, and it clipped my chin good and hard. She continued to roll over and slapped her palm across my cheek.

"Leave me alone! You son of a bitch, don't you ever touch me!"

"Fuck this, I don't have time for your tantrums."

"Where do you go at lunch, Bill?" Lisa asked, her face a tight mask of loathing. "You want to tell me that?"

"I go to Les's shop. We have lunch and play cards."

"No, Bill, you don't. I call the shop. No one answers. So, where do you go? Where are you in the mornings when you're supposed to be at the gym or at night when you're supposed to be working late?"

"Lisa, this is not the time. Didn't you hear what I said?"

"How long, Bill? How long have you been doing this to your family?"

"For fuck's sake, Lisa, there is a killer out there."

"I don't give a shit," she screamed. Tears were flowing freely from her eyes. "You've been *killing* this family, and I want to know how long it's been going on. Who is she?"

"I wish there was another woman, Lisa. I do. Then I could march her in here and maybe you'd stop poisoning yourself with those goddamn pills. Maybe you'd start caring about your daughters enough to spend time with them instead of curled up here in your fucking bed. But there is no other woman, Lisa. She doesn't exist."

"You fucking liar."

God knows, my behavior was not above reproach, but another woman had nothing to do with it. I thought about my daughters, alone in the car. They needed me. What was left of my wife wasn't going to leave, at least not with me. I backed away.

"Fucking liar," Lisa said through thick sobs, falling back to the bed and clutching a pillow to her face. "You fucking liar."

After setting my girls up in my office, I used the phone on Duke's desk to call State Trooper Coltraine. He'd left a message for me; the news wasn't good. His men found the bodies from the night before, from the rest area—three men, a woman and two little boys. Their remains were found about a mile into the forest.

"They were stripped clean," Coltraine said. "Hollowed out. Christ, Bill, I never saw anything like it. They were all laid out in a neat row...like a fucking buffet. You got any idea what kind of animal does a thing like that?"

Of course I had an idea.

"Look," I told him, "we still have that guy in custody, Sykes; the one we're certain grabbed Maggie. I spent some time with him this afternoon, and I'm sure he's connected to the murders. Maybe he has an accomplice, maybe more than one. You might want to get over here and haul him up to Marrenville to get some answers. I can't get much out of him."

More than anything, I wanted Sykes gone, but if that wasn't to be the case, then I wanted a good number of troopers on hand to help me fight off his enemies.

"I'll send a car," the trooper said. "We're still collecting forensics up here and we're running thin on manpower, but if your guy knows something, we'd better know it too."

"Any idea of when we can expect you?"

"A-S-A-P," Coltraine said.

I hung up the phone, sunset only minutes away. Where the hell was Les? My men were gathered in the front office, all of them looking at me like I was about to read off lottery numbers. Duke and Ed sat on the edge of a desk. Bucky sat in a chair. They wanted to know why I'd called all of them together. I needed to tell them something.

Shame and embarrassment will make you do a lot of stupid things. For instance, instead of warning everyone at the station what was coming down on us for fear of looking like a fool (after all I was going on the word of a lunatic), I instructed my men that we had word of a gang coming through town. Duke nodded his head, patted his holstered gun and kept gnawing on a toothpick. Bucky looked over the rim of his glasses, eyeing me like I was only slightly saner than the guy we had in back, and Ed said, "Usually, they just keep passing if you don't give 'em any trouble."

Ed was always shooting his mouth off. I should have expected him to question the thin story I laid out, but I was hoping my authority would carry it off.

When confronted with this logic, I embellished the story. "That would normally be true, Ed, but it seems our friend Mr. Sykes pulled some shit with one of their kids. They are coming here, and they're coming for him."

This seemed to work in the short term. Now, Ed too was nodding his head. On the plus side, my men would be at the ready, and if everything I believed, including Sykes, turned out to be wrong, I wouldn't go down in town history as the Sheriff two slugs short of a clip. On the bad side, none of us had any idea what to expect once the pack arrived.

I wanted to talk to Sykes before they did.

My daughters, Dru and Gwen, were playing in my office, busy fighting aliens on my computer. So, I told the boys to gear up with the shotguns—an order that made Duke's eyes twinkle—and I let myself into the holding area.

"Stupid fuck is out'a luck." Sykes said, his voice low and growling. The prisoner paced the cell, four steps forward and four back. He looked at the floor, his hands flapping against his thighs.

"I think you might be right about that pack."

"I might…be right. I might…be right," Sykes sang. "Is the cocksucker getting scared?"

"Watch your mouth, Sykes."

"Apology…scatology." The speed of his pacing increased. His palms swatted loudly against his jeans. Fingers clutched denim. Released.

"Look, I can't protect you if you don't tell me how to stop these things."

"Protect me? You'll be lining my belly before the night's out. Or one of theirs. Either way, you'll be sliding out instead of in."

"What are you fishing for, Sykes?"

He stopped pacing and spun on me. "Let me out of this fucking cell!" he cried, saliva spraying over his lips. "Let me out of here or I'll tell your redneck posse. I'll tell them everything."

"Why don't you just tell me how to stop this pack, instead of creating some sick fantasy about my personal life?"

"His scent was all over you last night, Bill." Sykes walked up the bars, grasped them in his hands. His fingers worked furiously on them like he was trying to draw milk from an udder. "There's no fantasy there. He arrived before you and that stink was on him. When you showed up it threw me, because the scents were so much the same. For a minute, I couldn't tell the two of you apart. You carried so many of the same scents as little Maggie's father, but you weren't him.

You'd been with him though. Oh, you spent a lot of time…
with him."

I checked over my shoulder to make sure the door to
the holding area was secured. "You don't know what you're
talking about."

"What is it, Bill? A quickie in a roadside motel once a week
so you can keep the evil beastie under control? Does he just
jack you off, or are you giving him the goods? Do you kiss
and coo? Do you like his taste? He's such a strong man, a big
man. Do you like Mayflower pinning you down and forcing
his cock in so you can pretend it's not what you want?"

"Shut your filthy mouth." My head swam in a tide of red.
I kept checking the door to make sure no one entered the
room. But what if they were outside, listening? I had to shut
him up. He didn't know anything about me, about my life,
about Les. He was a fucking monster. What in the hell could
he possibly know about it?

"Does he grunt your name when he's fucking you, or does
he call you 'baby'?"

Sykes smacked his lips loudly, making wet kissing noises.
He licked his lips, sending flecks of spittle to the ground.
Then he laughed, stepping back to the center of the cell.

I unclipped the holster restraint, grabbed the butt of my
gun. It seemed my skull had become a hive for swarming
wasps; they buzzed and stung, colliding in my head with fierce
agitation. My vision blurred. I paced the hall and fidgeted
madly, just as Sykes had done moments before, trying to get
myself under control.

My only clear thoughts were: *He has to shut up. Someone
will hear him.*

"Did it drive your wife into the arms of a real man, Bill?
Did it send her out looking for a dick that didn't taste like

Mayflower's shit? Or did she just drown herself in a few bottles of wine a night like my lovely dead bride?"

That was when I snapped. Twenty-four hours of turmoil churned to the surface, stabbing at my head and chest, leaving me enraged and irrational. My eyes filled with Lisa's angry face, her doped stare. Sykes was screaming at me, only it was Lisa's voice I heard.

"...*you fucking liar. I know, Bill. You think I don't, but I know. You haven't touched me in years. Not like a man would. Where do you go for lunch, Bill? Where do you GO?*"

I heard the shot even before I realized I had drawn my weapon. Sykes's body jerked to the left. He stumbled back and hit the wall. Behind me, a commotion rose at the door. Keys jangled, and Duke and Ed and Bucky shouted my name.

"Nice try," I said, holstering my weapon. Sykes glared at me from the back of his cage. I'd shot wide, aiming into the adjoining cell, where a cloud of dust from the wounded wall settled. The fucker could taunt me all he wanted, but he wasn't getting off that easy.

"Stupid Billy," he said. "Silly Willy."

Sykes slid down the wall and sat his ass on the floor, his legs splayed, his eyes staring blankly at the space between his feet.

The door to the holding area burst open. Duke and Ed pushed their way in, weapons drawn, while Bucky hung back a few steps and fumbled with the catch on his holster. Duke and Ed peered into the cell. It took them a bit of time to realize that our prisoner was not dead. They were all asking me what happened. My brain and heart were so beaten up by the last few minutes that I didn't have an immediate answer. Instead, I stumbled out of the holding area into the main office.

There, standing in the open doorway, was Les Mayflower.

◇

"Hey, Bill."

I was grateful to see Les unharmed, but he stood in the doorway like an accusation, a confirmation, and I had to look away. Even when I walked up to him at the door, I looked down, focused on our shoes pointing at the space between us.

"I never thanked you," he said. "For Maggie, I mean. Everything is just kind of jumbled up right now, and I know I was a jerk to you earlier. I didn't mean anything."

"It's okay," I told him. "But we've got some trouble coming this way. I need you to do me a favor, if you can."

"If I can," Les said cautiously.

"I want you to stay out of town tonight. Maybe go on out to the Comfort Inn in Charlesville. And I need you to take Gwen and Dru with you."

Les's face scrunched up in confusion. "What's going on, Bill?"

"I don't have time to explain it all, but please, just do this for me."

I walked away from Les toward my office where my daughters played. I opened the door, and my daughters looked up at me, wearing frightened expressions. They sat on the couch in my office, clutching at one another. I'd already forgotten about the gunshot. It must have terrified them. I hurried across the room, gathered them into a hug to let them know everything was going to be okay.

Another lie.

Les kept asking me questions. I evaded most of them, not wanting to frighten the girls any more than I already had. While I gathered up their things, I told Gwen and Dru that they were going to stay with the Mayflowers. That was their surprise, and it made quick work of relieving their frightened expressions.

"Bill, I don't know…" Les said.

I grabbed his arm, slapped the girls backpacks into his chest. He held them there with a big hand.

"Just do this. I'll pay for the rooms. Take Viv and the kids out to Charlesville. Call me in the morning, and I'll tell you everything."

"What about Lisa?"

All I could tell him was that I thought she would be fine.

I kissed my daughters, Dru and then Gwen, and I held their hands, leading them through the main office. Duke and the other men were milling around by the holding area, whispering to one another, falling silent when I caught their eye. A pang of worry flashed in my gut. Maybe Sykes had clued them in on our last conversation, but that didn't matter.

I could deal with the fallout if there was a tomorrow.

At the front door of the station, I knelt down for another kiss from my girls. "You two be good and do everything Mr. and Mrs. Mayflower tell you, okay?"

"We will, Daddy," they said in unison.

I was afraid to let them go. Honestly, I wondered if I'd ever see them again.

"I love you both very much," I said, hugging them to me tightly. "Now, let's hurry. Daddy has some work to do."

Les opened the door to the station house, still looking concerned. Over his shoulder I saw the vast marshy area spreading out from the street, the trees waving in the evening breeze.

And I saw the man running down the road.

And I saw the things sprinting at his back.

6

His name was Hugh Wrightley, and he didn't stand a chance. Hugh was a thirty-something graphic artist who worked up in Marrenville. He had a wife, a baby boy. I hoped they were still safe behind the locked doors of their home. As for Hugh, he was pumping his arms and legs as fast as he could, wasting no energy by screaming or checking over his shoulder. He'd probably never run so fast in his life, but it wasn't nearly fast enough.

Three of the things, from a distance looking identical to the beast I'd seen the night before, gave chase. Half a block up, one of the pack dove, caught Hugh's ankle with its hand and sent the artist crashing face first into the pavement. The three piled on him a second later.

Now, Hugh took the time to scream. Their animal faces buried in his back, ripping away cloth and skin and muscle amid low sprays of blood. Hugh's legs slapped the pavement, at first struggling but soon just convulsing spasmodically as death took him.

I searched the parking lot, scanning for any movement. The first thing I saw was Les's station wagon, and two frightened faces peering through the windshield. Viv and Maggie were not seeing the brutal disassembly of Hugh Wrightley, but they saw our expressions, and that was enough.

"Get them out of the car," I yelled at Les, already ushering my own children back into the station. "Duke, get Dru and Gwen back to my office."

My daughters were screeching, high and persistent. They backed away from the open door slowly, too slowly.

"Go on," I said. "Get in there. Duke will take care of you."

With that my girls scurried toward the open door of my office. Duke met them halfway across the room and scooped Dru into his arm, holding a shotgun in the other. He followed Gwen, scooting her along with bumps of his knee.

I looked back at the street and pulled my gun. The three beasts still worked over the man on the pavement, but they were no longer alone. The rest of the pack, some tall, some short, one stooped like a movie hunchback, gathered over them. At that distance, I saw them clearly enough. They were all extremely muscular. All were tinged in shades of gray from the old meat color of Sykes to a deeper, nearly charcoal hue. Their faces all stretched into elongated, fang-filled muzzles, and they were all looking at me.

Their leader was easy to pick out, just as he had been at the park earlier. Even transformed, he was striking. A shock of white hair rolled back from the canine face, draping like a mane over his rounded shoulders. His abdomen, flat and long and ridged with muscles ran up to vast pectorals, gray and smooth and heaving as if for breath.

I could not see his eyes from such a distance, but imagined they still held that expression of calculation, weighing the situation, planning the attack. We were fucked. I knew that then. Totally fucked.

Taking the lead, the alpha began a measured trot toward the station.

I checked on Les who was just pulling Maggie out of the car. Viv was still sliding across the front seat toward them.

"Come on," I called.

Les looked up with absolute terror in his eyes, but he had Maggie in his arms and Viv was climbing out of the car. The alpha was in a full run now. Already at the intersection, it wouldn't take but another handful of seconds for him to cross the lot.

I stepped out of the doorway, aimed my revolver at the charging creature. It veered sharply to the right and disappeared into the brush lining the lot. His pack was less strategic. They charged ahead.

I fired, clipping the side of a smaller one. It spun, roared, did an amazingly graceful sweep of its leg over the pavement and was back on its feet, running in less than three seconds.

"Inside," I shouted, firing again. The second bullet hit nothing, or if it did, had no effect. Les pushed past me, clutching his frantic daughter. Viv knocked me forward with her shoulder. Sent off balance, I squeezed a third shot and it ricocheted harmlessly off the concrete.

In four quick motions, I was back in the station, door closed, lock thrown. The room behind me was in chaos. Bucky and Ed were shouting questions. Les Mayflower and his family ran from one desk to the other, unsure where to go. In my office, Duke was trying to console my daughters, who were fighting with him, struggling to escape and run to me.

To serve and protect, right? Well, I started with the civilians.

"Les, get Viv and Maggie in the office."

He looked at me, confused and frightened.

"Get them behind a locked door. Duke, give Vivian your sidearm."

"She can't shoot," Les argued.

"She can if she has to."

Duke did as he was told, pulling his service revolver from his hip, releasing the safety and handing the weapon to Viv Mayflower. She hurried into my office and clutched the edge of the door. Beyond her, Gwen and Dru were holding Maggie to them as if protecting a sister.

Then the door closed, and they were gone.

"Bucky, give Les your shotgun. Go get another out of the cabinet. In fact get all of the weapons out. Pile 'em up in the middle of the room."

"What the hell is going on?" Ed called, already hunkered down behind a desk, his shotgun ready for a target.

"We're under attack. Get on the radio and call the state boys. Get them over here now!"

He gave me a concerned, uncertain look. Nodded his head.

Then the window behind me exploded, and I hit the floor.

Glass rained down on my back. Something heavy pushed against my shoulder blades driving me onto the linoleum. I cracked my chin, squirmed against the weight but it was already gone. Duke and Ed were firing their shotguns over my head. Les shouted my name. I rolled onto my back, caught a flash of something gray to my right, working its way deeper into the office.

The beast had two small swells of breast indicating a female. She bore down on Les, moving fast. Like the others, she was strongly built, moving lithely with cords of muscle flexing and relaxing in rhythmic motion. Her one full arm swatted the air as if trying to knock the buckshot from my deputies' shells to the ground. This beast used to be a beautiful young woman, a girl of Hispanic, possibly Native American descent—just a kid. But now she was something wholly different, a creature with lethal intent, and she was closing in on Les. In the corner by my office, he struggled with his own shotgun. I don't know if it was jammed or if he'd neglected to release the safety, but he had the barrel pointed at the ceiling and he was looking along the stock.

Another blast startled me. The beast fell sideways, hitting the ground hard, much of her ribcage caved. Les swung his barrel down and at point blank range blew the side of her head away, spreading a dark stain over the linoleum at his feet.

"Bill," Duke shouted. "Stay down."

A torrent of shots ran over my head. Ed was reloading but Duke was spraying the air above me. A moment later, Les joined him.

I crawled on my belly, past the reception desk and through the thigh-high door that separated the reception area from the office space. Once there, out of the line of fire, I got to my feet. They were swarming at the window. Gray bodies, one hardly discernible from the other for all of the movement, battled for space.

"What in the fuck are those things?" Ed asked.

"Don't ask," I said.

Ed looked at me like I'd just sprouted horns and a tail. "What do they want?" he asked.

"They want Sykes."

"Well, goddamn it! Just give him to them."

"It's a bit late for that," I said.

"Hey," Duke shouted. "They're gone."

I looked at the window, the wall around it pocked and ruined by buckshot, and saw that Duke was right. Through the opening, I saw the parking lot, the street, the marshland.

They were regrouping.

"Stay on your toes," I said. I had no doubt this was only a temporary respite.

Les worked his way across the office, staying low as he did until he bumped up against me. Bucky emerged from the hall, two shotguns resting across his arms. He also cradled three service revolvers and boxes of shells. Instead of taking a chance by walking in front of the open window, he crossed to the low wall, slid over Duke's desk, and moved slowly towards the rest of us.

The window in the hall behind him exploded. Startled, Bucky dropped all of the weapons and then did a strange little dance, as he fought to withdraw his sidearm.

A blur of gray flew through the window, hit the floor just across the divider. It shot a long-fingered hand out, grabbed Bucky's shirt front and then in a smooth motion whirled, flinging the young officer at the shattered window. His back snapped loud as a gunshot on the window frame. His legs, still whipping through the air, continued through the window. The momentum carried him out and into the hands and mouths of four of the pack, who disappeared with him a moment later.

It happened so quickly Bucky didn't have time to scream. We hadn't gotten off a single shot.

And the beast was gone, back through the window. The four of us remaining stared silently, trying to process exactly what had just happened.

"That's not real," Ed whispered next to me. "It's a trick."

"God help us," Les said. "Dear Lord, protect your children in this time of…"

"Les," I said. "Keep it together."

I crawled around him and retrieved one of the shotguns, started pushing shells into it. Duke shouted, "They're in the building," and began firing toward the hallway where the second window had shattered. From my place on the floor, I could hear the girls crying in my office. The sound of it tore me up inside. I'd been stupid bringing them here. I'd been stupid about so many things.

Once the shotgun was loaded, I set it down next to me and repeated the process. Then I loaded the revolvers and scooted the whole pile across the floor to where we had taken up our position. I didn't even see what Ed was doing until Duke shouted, "Get your ass over here and help us."

But Ed was at the door to the holding area. He figured he'd just let our prisoner out, give him over to the attacking pack. Problem solved. He already had his key in the lock. He was going for Sykes, not understanding that Sykes was already gone.

"Ed, don't go in there," I yelled. "That's an order!"

But it was too late. He slipped through the door. I could only imagine that the beast Sykes had become caught Ed near the bars. We heard his scream, high and shrill and brief, and then the disgusting, wet sounds of eating.

If we could get these damned things to pull back, to retreat even a little. I could go back there myself. I could pump buckshot into Sykes's head like Les had done with the first one. His death might be enough for the pack, though more and more, I doubted it. We weren't just enemies; we were food.

A shadow moved in the corridor. Duke and Les fired repeatedly at the motion, but the beast kept itself behind the wall, just out of range. The thing was smart. It was getting them to use up their ammunition.

"Stop firing," I said. "You're wasting your shots."

"How many of the fuckers are out there?" Duke asked.

"Eight," I said.

"No," he said. "I know I hit at least three of them in the window."

"Hitting them isn't enough."

"Dear Lord," Les said. "This is our punishment for breaking God's laws. Don't you see, Bill? Our abomination brought this down on the world."

"What the hell is he talking about?" Duke asked.

"Not sure," I said uncomfortably. "But give him a break. We can't afford to have him lose it any more than he already has."

"That's a lie," Les said. "A lie. You know what we did, Bill. You know our sin. We have to admit our sin and repent. We must accept his judgment."

"Les," I said with a sharp warning in my voice. "We do not have time for this. If your God is so pissed off at us that he'd kill all of these innocent people, then fuck him. My guess is, he has better things to worry about. Now, reload your rifle and shut up."

"I hate to break this up," Duke said, "whatever it is, but what are we supposed to do, Bill?"

"Go for the legs or the head," I told him. "Body shots don't slow them down much. If we get them on the ground we've got a chance."

"You think we can get those windows sealed up?" Duke asked.

"No. I honestly don't."

To prove my point, the stooped beast—the one that I imagined had been an old woman in her human form—flew through the opening and into the room as if launched from a cannon. She landed on the desk to our left, sending a cascade of papers and pens into the air over Les's head. He yelped and ducked low, rolled under the desk.

Duke blew out her ankle with a blast, sending her crashing to the desk. I moved fast. Got my barrel under her chin, saw the pain and fear in her eyes. I didn't allow myself to pity the old woman until after I pulled the trigger, sending most of her skull and its contents across the room.

"Good work, Boss," Duke said.

"Don't get cocky." I crouched down to check on Les.

He was curled up in the space, glaring at me. He looked around, surveying the underside of the desk, his gun held tight to his body.

"You okay?" I asked.

"Actually, I'm getting really pissed off."

His answer surprised me, but I was glad to hear it. I'd expected him to be babbling prayers or having a complete breakdown. It could have gone either way. The trauma could have sent him over the edge; instead, it pulled him a good distance back from it. I offered him my hand and half dragged him out from under the desk. He made it the rest of the way on his own.

"Duke," I said. "What have we got?"

"Still got the one in the hallway, maybe two. For now, they're staying away from the window."

That hallway was our weakest point. From where we were taking up positions, we didn't have a clear shot. Once the pack figured that out, they could enter through the window, gather back there and charge us. There were still seven of the beasts if I'd counted correctly. If even three of them tried that, we'd be so distracted the rest could easily slip in the front.

Glass crashed behind us. The sound came from the holding area, but that didn't have me too concerned. All of the cells had windows, but they also had bars imbedded in the concrete. Besides, if they got Sykes, it would buy us a little time. Maybe they'd be so enthralled with taking him apart, the rest of us could slip out the front.

The key was to get their numbers down. Right now, they could keep us surrounded, trapped in the station house. We might not be able to kill them all, but we had to start thinning the pack. At least then we'd have a chance.

We needed to have a man on the other side of the room divider, close to the front door. From there, he would have a clear shot into the hall, and maybe we could keep the beasts from gathering for a charge.

I explained the idea to my men again, figuring I'd be the one to cross that boundary. Duke spoke up.

"You'd better let me do it," Duke said. "No offense, Bill, but you're a lousy shot."

"No offense taken. You're right," I said. "We'll be able to cover the window and anything that tries to cross the reception area from the hallway. But they may go for the front door. If they break through that, you're going to have to get out of there fast."

"No problem."

Les and I took up positions behind the desk Ed had used, putting us just off center of the room. Duke climbed onto the reception desk and slid over.

He immediately began firing into the hall, and the first beast charged forward. He got the legs out from under it with a shot that blew out its knee. I took care of the rest. The second one leaped through the window cutting a diagonal line across the room, but instead of taking Duke off guard and flinging him out to the others, as they'd done with Bucky, the thing miscalculated. Overshot. It landed on the floor and slid into the reception desk. Duke rolled, aimed and blew a significant hole in its crotch, a second in its belly. It bent down, whether in reaction to its wounds or in an attempt to attack, I didn't know. Duke shoved the barrel of his gun up and fired. The shot took out most of the thing's neck, including the spine that held up its skull. It hit the floor with a moist slap.

Something odd happened then. Duke didn't see it from his position on the floor, and I don't think Les noticed. He was hurriedly reloading his shotgun.

The alpha male appeared, stepping from the shadows and into the light being cast from the office. His powerful torso was perfectly framed by the shattered window. His shock of white hair was disheveled and he had a deep wound along the side of his face. He looked in at me, eyes burning with intelligence and rage. He was done fooling around. I don't know how I knew it, but I knew it. He'd lost nearly half his pack in the last handful of minutes and still didn't have what he'd come for.

Slowly he looked from one edge of the office to the other, his calculating eyes taking in the interior terrain. Something caught his eye—my office door, I was sure—and his brows knitted tightly over his muzzle.

While a dread understanding of his intent settled on me—my children were behind that door—a bath of light rose behind him, making a halo of his white mane. He spun, dropped. The sound of a truck or SUV pulling into the lot was at once a relief and terrifying. I hoped that the passengers of that vehicle had seen what was waiting for them and drove the hell away.

Of course, these were the state troopers, finally come to pick up Douglas Sykes, and they weren't the retreating type.

7

The state troopers were going to die, I knew that. But their fight would buy us some time. I dashed across the room to the holding area, listened at the door but heard nothing. It was a thick, reinforced slab; so while it didn't exactly sound-proof the room beyond, it came pretty damned close. I'd been grateful for that earlier, during Sykes's rant, but now it was frustrating. I had no idea if the cell had held Sykes or not.

Only one way to find out.

I swung open the door. Ed lay on his back, his body jerking on the concrete floor. He wasn't alive. His face was torn away, his eyes gone. Sykes had dragged him close to the cell and was in the process of gnawing on Ed's leg. Seeing me, Sykes bolted upright. His long fingers wrapped around the bars, and he yanked hard. The bars didn't so much as creak. It would hold.

"Les, get over to the office door."

"Why? What's going on?"

"We've only got a few minutes. I want to get everyone back to the holding area."

"We'll be trapped back there," Les said.

"Look around, Buddy. We're trapped here. Just do it." Les looked uncertain but he agreed and set off toward the door of my office. "Duke. Come on back here. We need to give the state boys some cover."

Duke did as he was told but when he reached me, he didn't look happy.

"What's this all about?" he asked. "We're doing good out here. At least we know what we're dealing with now."

"That's the point," I told him. "Now that I know what we're dealing with, I see exactly how fucked up this whole situation is. Come on, the troopers won't last long."

Already the sounds of shattering glass and gunfire drifted through the open window. Duke and I approached it, guns ready. A low cry, that of a wounded man rolled in and I trembled. I kept my eyes peeled, searching the shrubs at the side of the building, making sure one of those things didn't leap out and toss Duke or myself into the night as they'd done with Bucky. The report of gunshots sounded outside. Men screamed.

"Jesus, Bill," Duke whispered.

Then I was in a position to understand his curse. Two of the beasts crawled through the shattered windshield of the state patrol cruiser. Two more flanked the vehicle and attacked through the driver and passenger windows. A bright flare of gunfire lit up the car's interior like a strobe light, briefly sending the squirming bodies of monsters into shadowed relief. The screams of men stopped.

I backed up and turned away from the scene. In the doorway of my office, Les was hugging his wife. The three little girls peered out around him. Dru caught sight of the dead beasts littering the floor and screamed.

"We gotta move," I told Duke.

"Here's how this is going to work," I said once I had everyone's attention. "Duke is going to lead you back through the holding area to the last cell. I want you all to get inside and push back into the corner away from the bars." I knelt down, looked at Dru and Gwen and Maggie Mayflower. "Girls, once Duke opens that door over there, I want you to close your eyes and don't open them again until you're where you're supposed to be. Mr. And Mrs. Mayflower will make sure you're okay." I didn't want any of them to see Sykes in his beast form, and I didn't want them to see what that thing had done to Ed.

My daughters nodded their heads, tears streaming down their cheeks. Maggie just bobbed her head once in a nervous expression of understanding.

"Okay, let's go."

I stood with my back to them, keeping an eye on the window, the door and the entrance from the corridor. They moved quickly. I was grateful for that. Gwen screamed again. Apparently she had not shut her eyes. It must have been terrible for her, but there was no other choice. If Sykes couldn't get out of his cell, then it was likely the others couldn't get into one.

At least that was my hope.

"Bill," Les called. He stood in the doorway, clutching the door. The rest of them were in the holding area. "Come on."

Giving the window one last look, I hurried to the door, feeling a sense of near relief. We could defend our location back there without surprises. I entered the holding area, closed the door and secured the deadbolt with my key. At my back, Les kept his gun trained on the beast in the first cell.

"That's it," I told him. "Let's go."

Les turned away from the cell, nodded at me. He should have kept his eyes on Sykes.

A muscular arm shot out between the bars and grabbed the barrel of Les's gun, yanking hard, throwing the man off balance. Les's foot slipped in a pool of Ed's blood, sending him into an erratic dance as he tried to keep his footing, but his ankle caught on Ed's arm, and he fell back, hitting the bars of Sykes's cell hard. I lunged for him, my only thought to get him away from there. Les scrambled to get distance between himself and the cage, but it was too late. Sykes reached through the bars, grabbed Les's shoulders and lifted him up.

Viv Mayflower and the girls were screaming. Duke ran from the back of the room towards us. Les was pale, dripping with sweat, his eyes as wide as a lunatic's.

I lifted my shotgun, but Sykes used Les's body as a shield. His swollen, canine face peeked out over my friend's shoulder. Duke stopped at the adjoining cell, unlocked it, slid inside to get a better bead on Sykes.

Before he could get a shot off, Sykes wrapped his hands around Les's face, one gripping his brow and cheeks, the other low on his mouth and jaw. He yanked with all of his force, tearing away Les's jaw and snapping his neck. Les stared at me, eyes cloudy, not yet dead. A tear ran down his cheek, traced over his upper lip and then dripped to his chest. He no longer had a chin to impede its progress. Then Sykes released him and Les fell to the floor like a sack of flour.

I fired wildly into Sykes's cell, as did Duke. The beast bounded, leapt, hitting the wall with his feet and hands only to spring across the cell, land on the cot and roll away. Back on his feet, he jumped nearly to the ceiling, spun and kicked out, launching himself from the cell wall across the chamber. We must have fired a dozen rounds into that cell, a confined space and at close range, and neither one of us managed to seriously wound the son of a bitch.

As a man, Sykes had wanted me to put a bullet in his head. The beast of him was desperate to survive.

A thunder rolled up in the holding area as strong fists landed on the door. The pack slammed at its surface with so much force it felt as if the building was shaking around us. Already, the hinges were creaking, working loose from the jamb.

"Bill," Duke shouted, "there's nothing else we can do."

But he was wrong. There was something I could do.

With all of my strength, I dragged Les's remains away from the bars. Gently, I placed him against the wall. Though I didn't know I was crying, one of my tears fell on his chest to stain his shirt. I touched his brow. A second tear fell. With less care, I yanked at Ed's leg, freed his foot from the bars and slid him across the corridor to join Les.

"Bill!" Duke insisted.

"Get back there with the others. I'm not done with this fucker yet."

Seething and barely able to think straight, I walked up to the bars. The beast crouched on the cot, panting, tongue lolling. I slid my key into the lock of Sykes's cell and turned it. Then I pulled the door open a crack and ran faster than I ever had in my life.

Sykes launched himself, slamming into the metal bars, sending them crashing back against the cell. In the corridor behind me, I heard his throaty growl, but I didn't turn back.

I sprinted toward Duke, who stood, eyes wide with shock, holding open the last door for me.

I dove into the cell like a Yankee needing home plate, slid across the concrete into the pile of people in the corner. Behind me, Duke slammed the cell door and leaped back.

"Are you out of your mind?" he bellowed.

Behind him, Sykes reached through the bars, swatting the air, reaching for whatever he could get his hands on, but soon enough, his attention was drawn to the clatter at the other end of the room. His hunters were nearly through the door.

Gwen and Dru wrapped their arms around me, buried their faces in my shoulders. Sykes grabbed the door and yanked, throwing all of his weight into it, but the steel didn't budge. Panicked, he turned away, ran halfway down the hall toward the door, then back. At the wall, in front of our cell, he fell to his knees and started beating on the floor. His force was so intense that he split his hands, leaving smudges of blood on the concrete. He scrabbled at the place with his nails. Pushed his head down and tried to gnaw his way into the floor. He was trying to dig his way out.

The door to the holding area came down and the pack filled the opening. The alpha entered first, his head high and regal. He looked down at the two bodies against the wall, checked the open cell on his left. Once he was certain of his surroundings, he set his attention on Sykes. They looked at one another for several moments, both loathing the image filling their eyes. The alpha moved first. He ran forward with such speed, I could barely track him. Sykes left behind his foolish escape plan. He crouched and then launched himself from the floor. He met the alpha in mid air. They collided and dropped to the concrete, the alpha landing hard on Sykes's chest. Clawed hands swatted the air. The alpha slashed and punched, while Sykes tried to protect himself from the blows. But the alpha had the superior position, slashing wounds in Sykes's shoulders and neck, landing fists on his brow and cheek and throat. With a garbled cry, Sykes's arms fell limp to the concrete floor.

The alpha leapt from the battered body. Sykes whimpered, and the pack was on him in a second.

I pushed my daughters' faces deeper into my shoulders so they wouldn't see what was to come. Even for a monster, the death was grisly.

The pack gnawed through Sykes's limbs, taking bits and pieces in their mouths, spitting them on the floor as if disgusted with the taste of him. Once his legs were gone below the knee and his arms snapped and shredded at the shoulder, Sykes could do nothing but rock back and forth on the floor, bellowing his pain. The smallest of the beasts, the Asian child, I thought, crept forward on hands and knees, slid between Sykes's flailing leg stumps and bit down hard, enclosing his genitalia with teeth and ripping the flesh free with a single jerk of its head. The alpha shifted his position and drove his fingers into Sykes's belly, ripping it open with a flick of his wrist. Then, this striking male was done with the source of his torment. He stood upright, chest out, looking down on the remains of his pack as they finished with Sykes.

Duke rose up with his shotgun, but I told him to wait. If destroying Sykes did not satisfy the pack, we could take up the fight. For now, they were distracted, their rage focused elsewhere. I saw no need to bring it back down on us.

They scratched and chewed at the torso, reducing the body to bone and mush. Heavy hands turned organs to pulp and muscle to shreds of dripping meat. The pack continued until nothing about Sykes was remotely identifiable, and still they worked the refuse of him. It was as if they expected to find a prize in the tissue, in the blood. But what they sought eluded them.

I understood, or thought I did.

They believed his destruction would free them from the nightmares, the violence, the uncontrollable transformations that pushed their humanity into subservience. It didn't happen. No miracle accompanied Sykes's murder. They entered this place, creatures torn between logic and compulsion. They would leave similarly afflicted, only with more faces to add to their scrapbooks of guilt.

The alpha turned to me. His muzzled face wrinkling with hate, his teeth bared in a feral display of rage.

The realization was upon him. His life was not changed, would never change. The bit of humanity trapped within the beast felt the disappointment, the crushing hopelessness. The beast only felt the pain. He roared at the ceiling. The sound could not be called a howl. It was too thick. Too garbled and tremulous. Too human.

The stench of Sykes's death—his mangled and opened bowels, his shredded bladder, pooling blood—rose thick in the holding area. Behind me, Viv Mayflower and her daughter sobbed over Les's murder. My daughters trembled, their breath hitching and panting, as if they'd recently completed a long run. Duke towered over us, his shotgun ready at his side.

In the corridor on the other side of the bars, the alpha turned to face us. His miserable voice now silent but his chest heaving with fury. Those eyes. His calculating eyes moved back and forth with slow regard, his gaze creeping over each of us. Pausing. Moving on to the next. I eased out of my daughters' grasp, sent them back to join Viv and Maggie. I lifted my own shotgun from the floor and stood up, shoulder to shoulder with Duke.

"He comin' in here?" Duke asked.

"No," I said. "He may try, but he is *not* coming in here."

The rest of the pack gathered over the remains of Douglas Sykes, muzzles and teeth and fingers dripping with his fluids and adorned with shreds of his meat. They were looking to the alpha, who was still looking at us. He gazed at Duke, then at me. Paused, staring deep into my eyes, seeing what I couldn't imagine. Fear? Anger? Some odd and muted sense of pity? He shifted his gaze away to look at the woman and girls behind me.

Then, the large and striking male with the shock of white hair lowered his head, and he stepped back. With a flick of his head, the rest of the pack retreated through the bent and broken door.

He followed a moment later.

"Shit," Duke said, his shoulders drooping. His whole body seemed to shrink, and the nose of his shotgun touched the concrete floor. He lurched forward, craning his neck to peer along the corridor into the office beyond.

"Get away from the bars," I told him.

He thought about it for a second, then returned to my side.

"You think they're coming back?"

"No," I said. I figured they got what they came for, and a good deal more. They'd achieved no release from the murder of Sykes; there was nothing else for them here except maybe a skull full of buckshot. That's the way I figured it. "But I've been wrong a lot today. Let's not take a chance that I'm wrong again."

So, Duke and I crouched down. I sat my butt on the floor, and my girls were on me a moment later.

"I wan'ta go home," Dru cried in my ear.

Gwen just held me tightly; her tiny arm a tight collar on my neck.

And we remained that way, close and scared, until morning came.

8

I was startled out of an uneasy sleep by my daughter. Dru stood over me, poking at my shoulder with her tiny index finger.

"I have to go potty," she whispered, looking around in embarrassment, her cheeks flushed red.

My eyes were gummy, so I blinked away the blurred edges. Daylight poured into the holding area through the glazed glass and the broken pane in the first cell where Sykes had spent his last night.

"Okay, Honey," I said.

I was still on edge, not quite ready to believe that sunlight necessarily meant safety. After all, there was no real reason to believe in any aspects of the legends I'd heard about growing up. No full moon. No crouched and hairy bodies. No silver weapons. Who could say if night meant any more to these creatures than rain or snow.

Duke grumbled when I tried to wake him, then he shot upright, slapping around on the floor for his shotgun. He saw that it was my hand shaking him and relaxed, wiping his eyes and letting loose a sustained groan.

"I'm clocking overtime," he mumbled. He got to his feet and scrubbed at his scalp with his fingers. Stretched, looked around.

In the back corner, Viv Mayflower was awake, staring with glassy eyes at us. Her daughter Maggie was asleep, using Viv's ample left breast as a pillow. Gwen was also asleep, curled up in a tight ball on the floor.

"Are we heading out?" Duke asked.

"Yeah, soon. Look, I'm going to check up front, make sure things are clear. When I give the word, I want you to carry Dru on back to the restroom. She needs to use the facilities."

"Daddy," Dru gasped, her cheeks blazing red.

"Sorry, Honey," I said with a smile. I was relieved that she could be embarrassed, something so simple, after the night she had endured. "Duke, I want you to lock the cell door behind you. I don't want those kids waking up and wandering through that mess in the hall."

"Got it," Duke said with a nod.

I unlocked the cell door, muscles tensed. In the corridor, I looked down at the ruins of Douglas Sykes, bits of white and pink showing through a sludge of red and black and brown. My stomach turned, but I kept walking, keeping close to the bars to avoid the bulk of the gore. When I reached the first cell, I closed the door. Out of reflex I looked over at the far wall at the remains of Les Mayflower, mostly hidden by Ed's body. Something cold dropped from my throat into my stomach and I stood taller, cocked the shotgun and walked into the office.

The body of an old woman with sagging skin was sprawled across a desk; a young woman, possibly Hispanic, perhaps Native American and missing an arm, lay on the floor in the corner. Both were motionless. I stepped through the low swinging door that separated the office from the reception area. Two more bodies. Both men. Both naked. Their faces and the backs of their heads blown away.

At the ruined window through a frame of jagged glass and masonry pocked by our gunshots, I looked out onto a slaughterhouse. A State Police cruiser sat on the gravel, battered, with its windows smashed. The remains of the men, along with the remains of Bucky Minden, littered the tiny pebbles. They had been stripped and devoured. A party of flies was already in full commencement, dancing and dipping in the cool dawn air. The insects were the only things that moved out there.

I wandered down the hallway along the front of the building, back toward the lockers, the showers, the restrooms and the shooting range, turning on lights as I went. Splashes of blood dappled the floor and shards of glass from the smashed window, but no bodies.

By the time I reached the door to the firing range, my heart was beating harder than a hummingbird's wings. But I opened the door and found the concrete alley empty.

Back in the office, I called for Duke, letting him know the coast was clear.

I took a step forward to meet my deputy and my daughter.

That's when the alpha struck.

I don't know how he got behind me, don't know what he used to crack my skull, but the scene before me blew apart, desks floating up and out of my vision, the ceiling warping downward to meet the floor. Filing cabinets bulging outward as if expanding with tremendous breath. All in a second. All in shades of gray. Then black.

I fell to the floor unconscious.

When I woke, the first thing I noticed was the pain. I tried to lift my head and it felt like my skull was lined with shards of glass, tearing my scalp and brain with equal ferocity. Closing my eyes against the agony, I pushed myself off of the floor, got my shaky legs under me and nearly crashed back to the floor. I fell against the divider for support, touched the wet wound on the back of my head and tried to figure out why I was in the police station.

Why were dead people littering the floor? What the hell was going on?

It wasn't until I saw Duke, lying face down by the holding area door, that the information I needed returned. The entire night before rushed back like a train boring through my skull, intensifying the pain in my head and the panic in my chest.

Dru?

In a fit of desperation, I searched for my daughter. I stumbled into the holding area, looked through the bars into each cell. Viv Mayflower was on her feet, holding Maggie and Gwen to her, looking terrified.

But Dru was not with them. The alpha had left me a message to that effect. I just hadn't noticed it.

I found the note pinned to the back of Duke's shirt just above a bullet hole and a smear of blood. The two words written on a scrap of paper worked their way into my head at first making no sense. I stared at the neat block letters, my mind so consumed with fear for my daughter's life that I couldn't understand what the note was telling me. As I tried to reason it out, a bolt of pain shot from the base of my neck over my crown to the bridge of my nose. Its intensity was startling, made the world go gray. But in its aftermath my head cleared and the two words suddenly made perfect sense: *The Park.*

Driving across Luther's Bend, painful emotions—terror and premature feelings of loss, and even guilt—took my mind away from the pain in my head. Around me, my neighbors, the people I had known all my life, went about their mornings. They made and drank coffee. Cooked and ate breakfast. Read the newspaper. Made love. Played with their kids. My head was not with them. I drove, as if through a tunnel carved in a desolate mountain. There was nothing but the entrance and the exit and all in between was cold and impenetrable, ultimately meaningless because it could not be changed.

I thought of how I might handle this situation, wondered what the alpha (because I was certain he was behind my daughter's abduction) would say when confronted. Maybe I was driving into a trap, but if the alpha wanted me dead, he would have seen to that back at the station, murdered me the way he'd murdered Duke.

No, he wanted something from me, and he was using my little girl to instigate the bargaining.

I turned onto Whitehall Road, my pulse tripping hard and fast as the park opened up on my right. I touched the butt of my service revolver, and then grasped it tightly. I held on as if it were the only real thing in the world, believing it could somehow keep me buoyed, save me from sinking into a black sea, churning with hateful emotions.

I stopped in the exact spot I'd parked the night Maggie was taken. Frantically, I searched the area for Dru, my eyes sweeping back and forth over the tree line, the grassy field and the lot of sand blanketing the playground. But she was nowhere to be seen.

Which is not to say that the park was empty.

As I'd suspected, the alpha was still in command. He stood by the Merry Go Round, dressed again in his casual businessman's attire: a navy blue polo shirt; khaki slacks. His white hair was combed and neat, but his handsome face and muscular arms carried a number of lacerations. He wore a serene, nearly pleasant expression. The icy calculation was gone from his eyes.

I walked over the grass toward the sandy playground, my hand again locked on the butt of my gun. The distance between us diminished quickly. With only a few steps left, I unholstered my weapon and aimed it at his brow.

He spread his arms wide and said, "Please."

"Where is she?" I demanded, sighting down the barrel at the man's brow.

"There," he said, lifting his left arm higher, pointing to The Den and the forest beyond.

I kept the gun against his head and looked to the wood. His pack was in there, with my daughter. I so badly wanted to pull the trigger and put an end to this monster. But I couldn't. The remainders of the pack might retaliate against Dru if I shot their leader down.

"Take me to her."

"That was always my intent," the alpha said, dropping his arms and turning slowly toward the forest. "My name is Bristol," he said. "You'll need that for your report. Tobias Alan Bristol."

"Duly noted," I said, barely able to control the trembling of my voice.

"I'm very sorry about what happened to your men."

"Sorry? I don't fucking believe you. You say you're not responsible—say you hate yourself. Well if that's true you could have blown your head off years ago when you realized what Sykes had done to you. But you didn't. You lived and you murdered and no one's to blame but you, so don't throw your apologies at me. They aren't worth shit."

"You don't understand," he said. "Dozens of times I picked up a gun, a razor, or stood on the edge of a skyscraper looking down. But the beast resists. I want to die, but it doesn't. I'm not like Sykes, Sheriff. I haven't enjoyed a minute of this hell."

"Just shut up and take me to my daughter, and I swear to God, if she's hurt, I will bury you and every one of those sick fucks with you."

"I assure you, Sheriff, that won't be necessary."

But I was the one deciding what was necessary. Once I had Dru safe and away from this place, I was coming back with a hunting rifle. None of these monsters was ever going to hurt another human being. I would hunt them down one by one if I had to. Whatever Sykes had begun, I was going to end.

We walked under the shadow of the tall pines, the cool morning air turning crisp and chill in the darkness. I reached out and grabbed the fabric at the alpha's shoulder, held tight while I pushed the muzzle of my gun into the thick white hair on the back of his head.

"You're a good man, Sheriff," he said. "I suspected that all along, but I knew it when you didn't shoot me on sight. You still have a strong sense of justice, of right and wrong. I regret the loss of these traits in my own character, but I've had to become far more pragmatic."

The forest fell in around us, dropping the temperature another couple of degrees. My ears were alert for any sounds in the wood, any indication that the pack was positioning itself for an attack.

"This has to end, you see," he said. "I'd hoped that Sykes's death would release us, and god knows how many others, but as you witnessed, that wasn't the case. Over the years, we've killed dozens like him, like ourselves. When we hunted, we killed cleanly so no more like us would rise and hunt."

"Quiet," I said. "I've heard more than enough."

We stepped into a narrow clearing, maybe two hundred yards into the wood. Lying on the ground were the remains of the pack. Four bodies, including that of the Asian boy, lay shoulder to shoulder on the ground, arms crossed over their chests. Long and ragged wounds were drawn across their throats. The arterial discharge painted their naked chests and shoulders crimson.

"You can see my sincerity," he said. "When we failed with Sykes, I saw no other choice. They fought me of course, but I was resolute. They're at peace now."

"And that just leaves you."

"Yes, Sheriff...just me."

"Well, why don't you take me to my daughter, and maybe I can help you find some peace of your own."

The alpha nodded his head and continued into the woods.

"It's the *maybe* that worried me," he said.

I wasn't paying attention to him, rather scanning the forest for any signs of Dru. I didn't understand how important what he had just said would be in the moments to come, how they would change my life forever.

"As I said, you're a good man. As a law enforcement officer, you're trained to apprehend. You only kill when threatened. How could I be certain that when the time came, you would release me? You see, I needed to be certain, Sheriff. I couldn't take the chance that you'd simply arrest me and let justice take its course. Because, as I said, this has to stop."

The alpha paused on the trail. He turned to me with a weak and pained grimace.

"Move," I shouted.

He nodded his head slowly, pushed aside a weak, brown sapling and showed me my daughter.

Dru lay on a bed of pine needles. Her eyes were closed but her face was taught as if haunted by a bad dream. Like the members of the pack, her arms were folded over her chest. And her neck was opened and painted with blood.

"I assure you she didn't suff..."

He never finished the sentence. I shot Bristol in the head, sending him onto a large, dead pine limb. Walking forward, I shot again and again. My body hummed with an energy that I thought would tear me apart, would burst forth exploding from my chest to disassemble me amid the woods. When I reached his body, I fired into his handsome face until my clip was empty. Then I used the butt of my weapon, beat him with it. Only violence distracted me from grief. In those moments, the world didn't exist. I didn't have to think about anything except lifting my arm and slamming it down with all the force I possessed. There was no family, no Dru, no deputies, no Les Mayflower, just the gun in my fist and the skin it tore, the bones it smashed and ultimately, the pulp it sank into.

Eventually there wasn't enough left of him—nothing recognizable remained above the man's neck—to assuage my misery. My shoulders ached and my palm was bleeding, and my daughter waited only a few feet away.

I went to Dru, knelt down, imagining that perhaps the man had tricked me, had merely knocked her unconscious and made her up to look murdered. I reached for any and all fiction, any soothing lie that would make my daughter alive and well. The whole time the energy in my chest built and built until I felt certain it would explode and kill me where I knelt, but there was no such relief.

I cradled my daughter in my arms. Tears burned along my cheeks, but I couldn't make a sound. Emotion clotted in my throat, paralyzed my chest. My mouth was open, trying to vent sobs and screams, but no such release was granted. Cruel imagination taunted me. Twice, I thought I felt a pulse coming from Dru's motionless body, and I pressed my fingers to her wrist, only to realize that the only heart beating in those woods was the one that strained, broken and aching, in my chest.

9

How do you go on when something like that happens to your child?

That was one of a dozen questions that played in a barbed loop through my thoughts in the days and weeks and months that followed my daughter's death. The other victims hardly concerned me, even Les. I was close to those men, considered them an extension of my family, but only an extension. Dru *was* my family, and she was gone, and how do you go on? I can't tell you. There are no words of wisdom here.

I woke up, wandered the house in a daze, and tried to protect the daughter that had survived, maybe tried too hard. Even Gwen's mother struck me as a threat, so I stayed home and close whenever I could. Lisa sank deeper into her addictions for a time. I suppose that was to be expected. We should have turned to each other for comfort, but the flimsy ropes and planks that bridged us emotionally had frayed and rotted long ago. Existing in the same house, united only by misery and our remaining, bereft child, we barely spoke to one another. What words we did exchange were often unpleasant.

We stuck it out together for eight months, and one morning I noticed that Lisa's eyes were clear and sharp. She did not go to the bottle upon waking, but instead went to the coffee pot, poured herself a cup and sat down at the table across from me.

"I hate you for what happened to Dru," she said. Her voice was calm and even tempered. She said it in the same way she might tell me the lawn needed mowing, or we were out of milk. "I don't want to, but I do. Some nights, I think about killing you for what you did. And then I think about why you did it, the way I was, and I think about killing myself instead."

"Lisa, I can't keep apologizing."

"You don't have to, Bill. I'm leaving. I should have done it a long time ago, long before the night she died. I don't know what you've been hiding, and right now, I don't want to know. I don't need to hate you any more than I already do."

And that was it. Later that afternoon, Lisa packed up the SUV and drove away, headed east to stay with her sister in Atlanta. She said goodbye to Gwen, kissed her and hugged her and then raced around the vehicle. She sped away, leaving our daughter sobbing in front of the house.

Gwen was to stay with me, and I was grateful. Lisa intended to enter a rehabilitation clinic when she reached Atlanta and didn't think she could manage being a mother during that time. She promised to call when she got settled and would send for our daughter when she was on her feet.

I haven't heard from her since.

As for the secret Lisa mentioned: well it isn't much of a secret, is it?

128

Everything Sykes suspected was, of course, true. Which meant that what Lisa thought was also true. She just didn't know the details.

I was with Les Mayflower for three years before the night our lives changed. We met at his shop for lunch or took weekend trips, told our wives we were fishing or hunting. So many times we talked about ending the relationship, especially early on. Days and weeks would pass, both of us struggling against it. Then one of us would call the other or we'd run into each other in town. Invariably we ended up on the cot at the back of his shop, needing each other in ways no one around us was likely to understand. Amid the shame and the guilt and thoughts of family and God, we found it impossible to let go of what we had.

Before Les…well, that doesn't really matter. He wasn't the first.

Sykes knew what I was going through. The monster was indulging in far darker needs than I, but he still understood the fundamental duality of my life.

I don't believe that I'm a monster, but I have lived like one. Secrets. Lies. The bitter emanations, drifting from a splintered soul, enveloping any and all close to it. For all of that, I'm guilty. The lunatic, Sykes, had little choice in the way he lived. But I do. I can recognize what lives within me and embrace it, casting off the façade, perhaps to ridicule, or I can go on as I have been, with the mask intact, bound in deceit.

You'd think it would be easy. I want it to be easy.

But I cannot claim an epiphany, can't tie things up nicely with a moral or a lesson learned. For now, I remain as I was.

Scared.

Ashamed.

Torn.